The Alpha Plague 3

Michael Robertson

Website and Newsletter:
www.michaelrobertson.co.uk

Email: subscribers@michaelrobertson.co.uk

Edited by:
Aaron Sikes - www.ajsikes.com
Terri King - http://terri-king.wix.com/editing

Cover Design by Dusty Crosley

Formatting by Polgarus Studio

The Alpha Plague 3
Michael Robertson
© 2015 Michael Robertson

The Alpha Plague 3 is a work of fiction. The characters, incidents, situations, and all dialogue are entirely a product of the author's imagination, or are used fictitiously and are not in any way representative of real people, places or things.

Any resemblance to persons living or dead is entirely coincidental.

All rights reserved

No part of this publication may be reproduced, stored in a retrieval system or transmitted in any form or by any means electronic, mechanical, photocopying, recording or otherwise, without the prior written permission of the author except in the case of brief quotations embodied in critical articles and reviews.

Would you like to be informed about my future releases?
Join my mailing list at:-

www.michaelrobertson.co.uk

Chapter One

Physically exhausted and still reeling from the shocking image in front of him, Rhys stared at the blood all over the police car and shook from his toes up. He reached out and rested against the vehicle for balance, the metal still warm from the day's sun. His head felt too heavy to hold up, so he looked at the ground as he drew deep breaths. Vicky had Flynn, but where the fuck had she taken him?

So much blood had been spilled inside the car that some of it had flooded out onto the road. It glistened in the fading sun. The smell of the diseased mixed with both the metallic reek of blood and the acrid tang of burning plastic from Summit City.

Several more deep breaths and Rhys gulped back the chemical taste from the fire. He lifted his head and looked around. There had to be a trace of Flynn somewhere; a trail they could follow. Thankfully, there didn't seem to be a trail of blood. Vicky would take care of him as she promised she would. But a near-stranger's promise offered little comfort to a father in need of his son.

Rhys had never seen the approach road so quiet. He'd only

used it in rush hour and now there would never be one of those again.

The door to the control booth for the drawbridge hung wide open. Rhys looked at the smoked Perspex windows. Maybe they'd been clear at some point before sweaty body after sweaty body had funked the small hut up. The unintentional frosting seemed to be years' worth of perspiration and dirt. A gap of about ten metres separated Rhys from the booth. Despite the distance, Rhys could almost smell the stale hut from where he stood. Fuck knows how people spent their days inside it.

Rhys looked across the river to see Summit City burning and could feel Larissa's attention on him. The press of her panic pushed into the side of his face like the heat from a strong fire, but he didn't have any answers for her. Their boy and Vicky were gone; what else could he say?

Rhys allowed the glowing horizon to hypnotise him and continued to watch the place burn. In a short time, the horrible city would be no more than ashes; maybe they'd be somewhere safe with Flynn by then.

The crackle of fire and pop of windows filled what would have been an otherwise quiet evening and was better than the screams of the diseased. He'd be happy to never hear *that* again.

With the shutters now retracted, the skyline once more stood as rows of tower blocks rather than phallic steel pillars. However, they weren't the tower blocks that Rhys had become familiar with; these stood windowless and charred as black smoke poured from the open spaces. The shining examples of commercial architecture were now no more than skeletal husks.

After a short while, Rhys' eyes stung and his vision blurred from where he hadn't blinked. The fire seemed to have done its job. Hopefully, it had killed all of the diseased including Dave. The poor man didn't deserve to suffer. None of them did. But even his thoughts of Dave seemed like a distraction. Something to take him away from the same question that repeated through his mind … Where the fuck was his little boy?

When Larissa walked over to Rhys' side, he tensed at her close proximity. He didn't need her aggression on top of everything else. He had no answers for her.

When he looked at her, she stared straight back, accusation in her green eyes. He said nothing.

After she'd looked from Rhys to the inside of the car and back to Rhys again, she spoke with such a sharp tone her words came out as razor blades.

"That's Oscar's axe?"

It seemed more like an attack than a question. How was it Rhys' fault? He took a moment to gather his thoughts. After a deep breath, he said, "Yep."

The panic of a mother, as justified at it was, hurt Rhys' ears as Larissa's tone became more shrill.

"*How* do you know that?"

"I watched him bury it into enough diseased faces."

"But it's just an axe." Rapid breaths rocked her frame. "It could be anyone's."

The sting of tears burned Rhys' eyes as his fear momentarily overwhelmed him. His boy was out there somewhere. He'd had everything he'd wanted and he'd fucked it all up when he went back into the city for Larissa and Dave. He shook his head.

"It's not just anyone's, Larissa. It's not a coincidence. Why do you think Vicky was running when we heard her?"

With wide eyes, Larissa dragged a hand over the top of her head and held her short black hair away from her face. She clenched her jaw and breathed through her nose.

"No, it can't be," she finally said. "There *must* be a mistake. I thought you trapped Oscar in the city."

"I thought so too, but that's *his* axe. I hope I'm wrong, but we need to plan for the worst so we're prepared."

Larissa's mouth turned down at the corners and tears glazed her stare as she looked from one of Rhys' eyes to the other.

"I *can't* plan for the worst. I *can't* do that."

With a hand on Larissa's slim shoulder, Rhys squeezed it and said, "I don't mean we should plan for Flynn to be …" The hot lump in his throat cut his words off. "Well, what I mean is that we need to plan for Oscar to be out of the city. Not for anything to have happened to Flynn. We've just heard from Vicky, so we know he's okay at the moment."

Before Larissa said anything in response, Rhys' grief overwhelmed him and his vision blurred. He looked at the burning city again.

"I thought I knew fear, and then we had Flynn. Now there's someone out there who I care infinitely more about than I do myself, and I have no control over his wellbeing. After everything that's happened today, I *can't* lose him. I can't even entertain the idea of that. We'll make sure we save him … I promise."

Larissa's grief turned to rage in a flash and her eyes narrowed. "Forgive me if I don't put much faith in one of *your* promises."

"What's *that* supposed to mean?"

"Do I need to spell it out? You're a *liar* and a *cheat*. You talk about how much Flynn means to you, but you were happy to fuck around when he was just a baby."

The little strength that remained in Rhys' body left him. He pulled his hand away from Larissa's shoulder and leaned his entire weight against the car again.

"I promised Flynn I'd rescue you."

Stumped for a second, Larissa came back at him. "But that doesn't mean you had to leave him with *her*."

Like he could have done anything else. Rhys opened his mouth to reply, but Larissa didn't give him a chance. Instead, she stepped forward and punched him on the front of his right shoulder.

"Why did you leave our boy with a *complete* stranger? You wonder why I fought you for custody of him? The first time you look after him in years and *this* is what happens! You're a fucking liability."

The lethargy of just seconds before left Rhys as adrenaline surged through him. He stood up straight, balled his fists, and pulled his shoulders back while he stared directly at her. His shoulder stung where she'd hit it.

Larissa didn't back down, her scowl as fierce as ever.

With a clenched jaw and a raging pulse, Rhys stared at the woman he once loved. "So that was why you kept him away from me? And there I was thinking it was just you being a cunt."

"I wasn't the one who fucked someone else, Rhys."

"Do we have to keep going back to that?"

"Yes, we do. If you could have kept it in your trousers, then we would be in a *very* different place by now."

"So the zombie apocalypse has hit because *I* had an affair?"

"You know what I mean." Larissa then turned her back on Rhys and looked out at the city.

With only the back of her head to look at, Rhys glanced down at the axe in the car. His heart rate increased as he stared at the savage weapon. To touch the thing would be to connect with Oscar more, but maybe he could use it just once. He could bury it into the back of Larissa's skull and tell Flynn she never got away. A shake of his head banished the fantasy.

Rhys may have been many things, but he wasn't a cold-blooded murderer. Despite their dysfunctional relationship, she'd always be the mother of his child.

"I left Flynn with Vicky so I could come back into the city to rescue you. How many times do I have to tell you that?" Just the thought of it clawed at Rhys' heart, but he said it anyway. "The first thing he said after I'd rescued him was 'where's Mummy?' What else could I do? I love that boy, despite what you think, and I want to do everything I can to make him happy. Yeah, I fucked up, but that doesn't mean I love him any less. I didn't want to leave him but I couldn't stand to see him so upset."

Because she only had one shoe on, Larissa stood at an angle when she looked back at Rhys and folded her arms across her chest.

"So you would have left me to die?"

Rhys didn't respond.

"That wasn't a rhetorical question."

Rhys still didn't respond.

After she'd released a heavy sigh, Larissa shook her head. The fury seemed to leave her as her frame sagged.

For a few seconds, neither of them spoke. The thought of trying to rescue their son with her riding on her moral fucking high horse filled Rhys with dread, but at least now she knew the truth of it. Rhys saved her because of Flynn, not because he wanted to. She had no leverage with him. If she died, she died; he'd done his best.

Unable to look at her any longer, Rhys looked back over the wide river at the burning city. Both the smell and taste of molten plastic hit him again as he stared at the black smoke.

Rhys then leaned into the car and the rotten metallic reek of the diseased hit him with a hot uppercut. When he put his hand on the seat to lean in farther, the blood oozed up from the fabric and soaked in between his fingers. He grabbed the radio's black microphone and pulled it toward him. The curly flex tugged back, and with his hands so slick with blood, Rhys had to grip harder to keep a hold of it. He pressed the button on the side.

"Hello? Vicky?"

The hiss of white noise answered him.

"Hello?"

Nothing.

"Hello?"

Still nothing.

"Fuck!"

Rhys threw the microphone back into the car again. "Fuck it!" When he looked down at the ignition, he saw the keys had gone too. Not that he had any particular desire to drive the thing in its current state.

Larissa chewed her bottom lip as she watched Rhys. "We

need to do something. We need a plan. I don't know about you, but there's no way I'm going to stand around and wait for your new girlfriend to come back."

Rhys opened his mouth to reply but he stopped dead. The hairs on his arms rose as he looked in the direction he thought a sound had come from. Then he heard it again, louder than before and loaded with rage. The screams of the diseased.

His heart kicked like it wanted free of his body and the back of his throat dried. "Oh fuck."

When he looked at Larissa, he saw her frozen to the spot with her mouth open. A shudder snapped through him. "We need to get the fuck out of here. Now!"

Chapter Two

Eighteen months ago

The soft leather of the huge armchair creaked as Vicky sank into it. She may have had to spend time with her brothers and their obnoxious offspring, but at least she got to enjoy the luxury they always expected in their lives.

The waiting room served just four private rooms, unlike the areas used by the general public, which catered for the rest of the large hospital. Instead of rows of seats placed so close together you rubbed shoulders with your neighbour, each seat in this waiting room had a clearance of at least one metre on either side. Even with the extra space, Vicky still decided to sit on the opposite side of the room. The last time she'd been in a room with her brothers, they'd argued for about an hour before they finally decided she should be the one to look after their mother as her health declined. They both had families, so of course Vicky had to do it. Never mind that she couldn't stand the bitch.

One other family huddled in the corner; a man and two

young boys. The dad hugged the boys as the three of them cried quietly. If Vicky were to guess, she'd assume the mother of those boys didn't have long left. A pang of grief twisted her heart. The kids seemed so young and the dad so lost.

The shrill call of Austin, Mike's boy, sent needles into Vicky's ears and snapped her entire body rigid. The dad and the boys in the corner barely noticed it. At least the overwhelming grief had numbed them to the point where the precocious little shits didn't bother them. Not that Austin could do much about the noise. At four years old, he could hardly be expected to manage his behaviour. Mike should take that responsibility.

Mike called across the room to Vicky. "What's wrong with *you*?"

When Vicky looked up, her face ached from her hard frown. "Huh?"

"You're looking at my boy like he's an animal."

Vicky's cheeks flushed hot when she looked at the family in the corner. Their faces limp with grief, they stared in shock at the interaction between her and her kid brother. A child they could seemingly ignore, but fully grown adults ... they should know better.

A deep sigh and Vicky shook her head before she looked down at her lap.

"Don't ignore me. You're only in this room because Max and I have paid for it. How *dare* you look at our kids like they're a nuisance!"

As Mike spoke, Jacob, Max's eldest son walked over to the confectionary counter and asked the person behind it for his fifth fizzy drink. The previous four stood lined up on the window ledge, each one still over three-quarters full, and each one glowed a different neon colour. No wonder the little brat had ants in his pants and a waistline bigger than Vicky's.

Ed, Jacob's younger brother, appeared behind him and asked for two more cookies. He'd had six in total and Austin had eaten three. All the while, Max and Mike either glared at Vicky or spoke so quietly she couldn't hear what they said. It had been that way since their dad died. The second the first shovel-full of dirt hit the top of his coffin, Vicky got shoved to the family's periphery—unless her mum had felt particularly venomous that day; then she was front and centre. At least once a week, the family would turn on her as a unit and pull everything about her apart. Everything from her clothes, to her hair, to her weight. The slut of the family, she caused nothing but trouble. If only her mother had died before her dad. How different things would have been then.

A nasty sneer twisted Max's face when he looked over at Vicky. "What is it? Do you think you're something special? You sit over in the corner on your own as if your shit don't stink."

The dad in the corner flinched at the swear word.

After she shook her head, Vicky looked away from her brother.

"You *clearly* do. You've always thought you were the golden child. Daddy's little princess, you couldn't do anything wrong in *his* eyes."

The dad in the corner whispered something to his boys and the three of them got to their feet and left.

After they'd closed the door behind them, Vicky stared at Max. "They left because of *you*, you know. When will you learn to keep your fucking mouth shut? I just want to be here for the end of Mum's life, although I don't know why, and then I'll be gone. I promise you, you'll *never* hear from me again."

"I hope you don't expect to be left in Mum's will," Mike said.

Vicky drew a deep breath to respond and then sighed. There didn't seem to be any point.

"So what is it?" Max asked. "What is it that makes you think you're so fucking special?"

Vicky stared at the ground. Highly polished wood, it didn't look like it belonged in a hospital. The smell of coffee from the machine in the corner made it feel like a high-end café, although the undercurrent of disinfectant remained as a permanent reminder of exactly where they were.

"Come on, Vick," Mike said. "Enlighten us. Why are *you* so special?"

"I don't think I'm special," Vicky said. "I was just never a part of things after Dad died. Your little clique with Mum pushed me away, so I chose to stay away. And the reason I'm over here now? I don't want to sit with your children. That's fine if you don't want to teach them manners, but I'm not being associated with them."

"They're *kids*," Max said.

Vicky watched Jacob jump onto one of the comfy armchairs before he launched himself off it again. His flat feet slapped against the hard floor with a *crack* that snapped through her.

"Jacob's *eight*. Eight is old enough to know better. Even a four-year-old should be encouraged to behave appropriately. But it's *your* parenting I have a problem with, not their behaviour. I wouldn't expect anything else from them if they're allowed to run wild."

Mike stood up and pointed down at Vicky. "What the fuck would *you* know about raising kids? You haven't had a boyfriend in years, let alone even thought about having a family of your own. I think I'll get my parenting advice elsewhere, *thanks*." Before he sat down, he said, "We paid for this suite so Mum could be comfortable in her final days, so maybe you need to start appreciating that rather than criticising us like you always do."

"Did you pay for this room? Oh, forgive me! You've only mentioned it *fifteen* fucking times. Thanks for reminding me. Besides, you give it the big *I am*, but who's looked after Mum for the past few years while you two have got on with your lives?"

Max stood up next to Mike, but before he could speak, a nurse emerged from one of the care rooms and cleared her throat. "Um, I think it's time."

Silence fell over the room and the three siblings stared at one another. After a deep breath, Vicky nodded and they all followed the nurse through.

***

The nurse held the door open and Vicky entered last; there were no gentlemen in her family.

The second she stepped into the lavish room, the smell of death and disinfectant hit the back of her throat. It left a chemical taste on her tongue and stirred nausea in her guts.

Even now, with the old woman frail and decrepit in the bed, Vicky's nerves set on edge. With her grip on life so tenuous, the old witch still looked like she could sit up and give Vicky one final onslaught of abuse.

As always, Max and Mike rushed to their mother's side. They each took a hand and both stared at their momma bear. Vicky remained on her feet at the end of the bed and looked down at the skinny woman.

The boys, Jacob, Ed, and Austin, ran over to the free vending machine in the corner. Jacob went first and punched in a code that delivered him yet another radioactive-looking fizzy drink. The white metal spiral twisted and pushed the soda forward until it hit the collection tray at the bottom with a loud *thud*.

Where she had once had tubes up her nose, Vicky's mum now had an oxygen mask strapped over the lower half of her face. Were it not for the slightest movement of her chest, Vicky would have called the private ambulance already.

The ECG machine pipped in the corner as Vicky looked at it and imagined the flat line. Not long now.

"Oh, Mum," Max said. Tears streaked his cheeks and his face buckled. "I love you, Mum. We're here now. Mike and I are here, it's okay for you to move on."

Although she had her eyes closed and looked as if she had nothing left, Vicky watched her mum squeeze the hands of both of her brothers. A rattle, like something flapped in her throat, came from the old crow's chest and she loosened her grip.

Social convention dictated that Vicky should speak at that moment. Fuck social convention. The old woman had taken enough of Vicky over the years, she didn't deserve any more. But Vicky didn't leave. An important and hideous chapter of her life neared its end and she needed to witness it.

Unlike Max, Mike couldn't speak. His mouth turned down in a strong frown and a constant stream of tears ran down his face.

A fight broke out by the vending machine. Vicky looked across to see that Ed had ordered the last of one of the fizzy drinks, and Jacob had taken it off him. The fat little shit seemed determined to sample every bottle of soda known to man, and family or not, his little brother wouldn't get in the way of that.

Max's voice snapped through the room. "Boys!"

They froze.

"Behave!"

At that point, Ed gave up on the drink and returned to the vending machine. Only a couple of sips into his current soda, Jacob placed that one on the side and opened the one he'd stolen from his brother. The pair glared at one another while Jacob sipped on his new beverage, spat his mouthful back into the can so no one else would drink from it, sipped on it again, and grinned.

Vicky looked back at her mum. Her strained breaths slowed a little and the gap between inhale and exhale grew each time. Vicky's mouth dried as she watched on. The temperature seemed to rise in the room. Her brothers continued to sob like the babies her mother had created.

And then, just like that, her next breath never came. A second later, a continuous buzz issued from the ECG machine.

Max grabbed the call button next to her bed and pressed it repeatedly. Mike wailed and dropped his face against their mother's corpse.

Vicky stared at her mother for a moment longer. She then

spun on her heel and left the room.

Three nurses and a doctor rushed past her through the waiting room, but Vicky kept going.

The woman had died.

It was finally over.

***

An emptiness sat in Vicky's gut that spread through her entire body. Numb and hollow, she stood in line in the hospital's coffee shop and stared through unblinking eyes. The hiss of steam, the white noise of people's chatter, and the smell of coffee, all of it seemed deadened in some way as the death of her mother settled in.

She should be glad to see the back of the old witch, but happiness didn't enter the equation. After a lifetime of simmering resentment from her, and then overt resentment after her dad had passed, Vicky still couldn't feel relieved that she'd gone. The image of her brothers' faces as they grieved ran through her mind. The pair of them made her skin crawl, but she loved them. As much as she didn't want to, she had an attachment to the two obnoxious pricks. One day she'd work out how to switch that off. Maybe at the funeral she could put it all to rest … if she chose to go at all.

The queue moved along and Vicky shuffled forward with it. The man behind the counter spoke. She could see he'd spoken because his lips had moved and he stared straight at her, but Vicky hadn't heard him. A shake of her head and she said, "A large gingerbread latte, please." That must have been what he wanted to know. Why else would he talk to her?

When Vicky wiped her face, she realised her cheeks were soaked. Tears ran down them. Tears she didn't feel or have any control over. It was almost as if her body had taken charge. Like it needed to force her to grieve so she could exorcise the demon that was the impact her mother had held on her life. She'd have to cry for decades for that.

With a shaky hand, Vicky pulled several napkins from the holder on the counter and wiped her face. When she opened her bag to retrieve her purse, a large hand gripped her forearm.

Her pulse skyrocketed when she looked up and saw the man. Well over six feet tall and with sharp blue eyes, he offered her a sympathetic smile.

"Let me get that for you, love."

Vicky shook her head. "Um … no, it's fine. Thank you. I'm fine thanks. I'll get it."

The man kept his kind, yet assertive grip on Vicky's forearm and handed a ten-pound note to the guy behind the counter. "I *insist*. You look like you've had a rough day."

The dam in Vicky's heart burst and her grief rushed forward. Unable to speak, she nodded at the man. She then moved across to wait for her coffee.

After the tall man ordered his drink, he nodded over to a corner seat. "It looks quite secluded over there. Why don't you go and sit down and I'll bring your coffee over to you?"

With her brain scrambled from the day's events, Vicky still didn't have any words. She nodded at the man and walked over to the seat he'd pointed at.

***

In the couple of minutes that passed while Vicky sat at the table, she'd managed to pull herself together somewhat. She'd stopped crying and dried her face with the handful of napkins she'd taken over with her.

The two large coffee cups looked small in the man's hands as he walked over to the table. He placed Vicky's down and smiled at her. "A stupid question, but are you okay?"

A tremble stirred in Vicky's bottom lip and she bit it to keep it in place. After a deep breath, she nodded. That's all she'd done so far. In the face of this man's kindness, she'd turned into a dumb parcel shelf dog. She cleared her throat and said, "Do you want to sit down?"

The man shook his head. "No, I don't want to intrude. Whatever it is, you look like you need some time on your own."

Another deep breath and Vicky sighed. "It's fine. *Honestly.* Please, sit down."

The chair screeched over the laminate floor when the man pulled it away from the table as he sat.

"I'm really sorry," Vicky said. "Look at the state of me. I'm a mess."

The man batted the comment away. "So what's going on? Do you want to talk about it?"

Just the thought of the words made Vicky's eyes sting and her throat ache. "My Mum …" She stopped for a moment, took a deep breath, and used a napkin to dab her leaking eyes. "My Mum … she died today."

The man reached across and grabbed one of her hands. Vicky looked down at his soft yet firm grip and her heart fluttered. Normally, the action would feel out of place. She'd only just met the guy after all. But he had a way about him, something reassuring and kind. The warmth and strength he held her with felt safe.

"I'm *so* sorry," he said.

"Don't be. I *hated* her."

The man balked and his azure eyes widened.

"I know … callous, right? It's strange that I'm crying. The woman did nothing but make my life hell. She tormented me for years. She and my brothers emotionally abused me, yet here I am crying for the old bitch. Families are fucked up, eh?"

The man didn't reply. Instead, he stared at Vicky, a slight frown of compassion as he allowed her to speak.

Vicky shook her head and wiped her eyes again. "Listen to me pouring my heart out to a complete stranger. I'm *really* sorry. I'm Vicky, by the way."

The man squeezed her hand. "Honestly, you've *nothing* to be sorry about." His smile broadened to show off two rows of perfectly white teeth. "I'm Brendan."

Chapter Three

The road by the drawbridge was a seven-lane highway. The police car sat in the middle of it so exposed it only left the pair one place to hide. Rhys grabbed for Larissa's hand and, in his haste, missed on the first attempt. On the second try, he grabbed a hold of her and dragged her over to the control booth for the drawbridge. She followed him with a ridiculous limp since she only had one shoe on.

En route to the booth, she stopped dead, which in turn snapped Rhys to a halt. Just before he could berate her, she lifted her foot, tore the shoe off, and threw it on the ground.

The screams grew louder and Rhys stared at the horizon. The brow of the hill may have hidden them but the fuckers were close. He gripped Larissa's hand harder than before and continued toward the drawbridge's control booth.

The light metal door shook when Rhys yanked it open. It reminded him of the kind of doors used on the cheap caravans he'd stayed in as a kid. As floppy as wet card, Rhys had seen more robust tin foil. The whole thing buckled again when he tugged it open wider, including the large Perspex window. As gross as the frosted panes looked, whether dirty or designed that way, they'd work in Rhys and Larissa's favour once they got inside the small hut. Anything to give them a better chance to remain hidden, if the diseased saw them before they got inside the booth … he stopped any further thoughts. A chill snapped through Rhys. It didn't bear thinking about.

Rhys stood aside to let Larissa in first and watched the brow of the hill as she hid on the ground. He heard the clumsy patter of feet join the cries of the diseased. Impatience coursed through him and forced him to tap his foot as he waited.

It only took a few more seconds for Larissa to make herself comfortable, but it felt like an age passed as Rhys divided his attention between her and the sounds just metres away from them.

The second Larissa settled, Rhys stepped in and held his breath as he pulled the door to. Fortunately, the flimsy thing made little sound as he tugged on it. He then slid down next to her and leaned his back against one of the warm walls. After he'd pulled his knees up to his chest, he wriggled to try to find comfort on the cold concrete. Adrenaline roared through his system and pulled everything tight as he sat there and looked up at the dirty window. Any moment, a wounded and enraged head could fill the cloudy space. Rhys tried to shake the thought from his mind. Everything would be okay. It had to be.

The booth reeked of old sweat and flatulence. It had also captured the day's heat and held onto it much like an unopened tent would. Sweat itched along the back of Rhys' dirty neck.

Once inside, Rhys couldn't hear anything other than the sound of his and Larissa's ragged breaths. Although the booth hid them from the diseased, he had to deal with his muted senses because of it. With less awareness of the monsters outside, they could be ambushed at any moment.

Larissa hid beneath the control desk with a tall stool next to her. Topped in faux black leather, it looked as neglected as the rest of the booth. A huge tear ran around the outside of the cushion and a wedge of foam poked through like a dog's tongue on a hot day. Although still chrome, the stool's base had caught rust as if it were a disease. Flecked over every part of it, the brown dots dulled the shiny finish.

Crammed in so close Larissa's knees pushed into the side of his thigh, Rhys wriggled again. If anything, it made the hard ground even more uncomfortable and his bum had already turned numb. When Larissa moved, she nudged the seat by accident and its legs scraped across the concrete. The screech accelerated Rhys' pulse and he held his breath as he listened for a reaction outside.

After a few seconds none came, so he continued to look at the stool. They should have moved it out before they got in. It took up too much room.

From his vantage point on the ground, Rhys could see what seemed to be years' worth of chewing gum stuck beneath the desk. A few pink blobs had been wedged to the bottom of the stool too.

The murky window that faced the police car sat low enough for Rhys to be able to see out of it. He'd had to stretch his back a little, but it gave him a decent view of the top half of the vehicle.

Another shift to try to find comfort on the hard and dirty

concrete and Rhys watched the car. Sweat turned his back slick and a shake wobbled his hands.

"I'm scared, Rhys," Larissa said as she remained curled in a ball on the ground.

"I know. I'm scared too. But everything will be okay."

"How the fuck will everything be okay? You've left our son with a lunatic."

After a deep sigh, Rhys closed his eyes for a second. He then looked down at Larissa beneath the desk. "That's going to get old *very* fucking quickly. And is now *really* the time?"

Almost as if she'd forgotten herself for a moment, Larissa raised her voice. Her nostrils flared and her red, sweaty face turned a deeper shade of crimson. "But it's true!"

Rhys balled his fist as he frowned down at his ex-wife. "What the fuck? Why don't you just go outside with a sign that says 'zombie bait' on it? Shut the fuck up."

Larissa's face reddened to the point where it looked like she'd pop as she glared at Rhys. She ground her jaw, but she kept her mouth shut.

After he'd tugged at his collar, Rhys let it settle back against his itchy neck. If anything, it made the discomfort worse than before. He fanned his face with his palm and the very slight movement of air helped cool his skin just a fraction. "I know things seem really fucking desperate right about now, but we need to have faith. We can only control our intentions, so let's put everything into that and believe that things will work out fine."

Before Larissa could speak, Rhys heard the snorts and groans of the diseased and glanced outside again. Unable to see all the way to the brow of the hill, they still remained hidden from him. He lowered his voice some more. "Vicky said we could trust her."

"And you've chosen to?"

Another glance outside. "Keep your voice down, yeah? If they hear us, we're fucked in here."

Never one for being told what to do, Larissa glared at Rhys again.

"I don't think we have any choice *but* to trust her," Rhys said. Anxiety fluttered through him. Truth be told, he didn't trust Vicky one bit. She'd lied to him and was connected to the Eastern terrorists in some way. He could only guess at what that connection was. But he couldn't show Larissa his true feelings. Besides, he needed to have faith since he didn't have anything else to lean on.

Rhys looked back down at Larissa as she brushed her black hair away from her forehead. "Do you have any other alternatives?" he asked.

Larissa drew a deep breath as if to launch into a tirade, but when the screams of the diseased grew louder, it stopped her dead.

Rhys straightened his back and peered out of the window. Seven of the horrible fuckers came into view as they ran, full tilt, for the police car.

Larissa shook next to Rhys. She breathed rapidly and whimpered.

The first four of the diseased made it to the car and stopped. They scanned the area with their usual jerky head movements. Their glazed eyes seemed to look for changes in light rather than anything specific. Surely they only had a limited field of vision. They returned their attention to the car.

Rhys had left the driver's side door open, so one of the diseased stuck its head in and sniffed, at least that's what it seemed to do. From his current position and through the murky window, Rhys couldn't be one hundred percent sure.

Rhys' heart now beat so hard each thud rocked him where he sat. His mouth had turned dry in the humid booth and a stale taste lay along his tongue. He swallowed several times as he watched the diseased in the car lean farther forward and rest its hands on the driver's seat. Rhys looked down at the dried blood on his own hands from where he'd done the same. It had formed a taut crust over his skin.

The diseased pulled back out of the car and held up its hands. For a second it simply stared at them as they glistened in the fading sun. It then looked up at the sky and roared so loudly the entire world seemed to freeze in reaction, Rhys included. Not a call to action, the roar spoke of a broken spirit. It spoke of grief for a loved one. It spoke of a brotherhood or sisterhood that ran deeper than most human connections, almost as if the thing itself had been hurt.

In response, all of the other diseased copied the action. Diminished compared to the first, the sound still set the evening air alight with rage. As one, they descended on the abandoned car. In an uncoordinated melee, they threw slaps and kicks at the vehicle. The bodywork boomed from each blow. Then they pushed and rocked it as if they could turn the thing over.

Rhys' stomach clenched as he watched the feral behaviour. He looked down at Larissa, who lay on the ground with her eyes wide and her mouth slightly open. He couldn't explain what he saw to her because any noise could give them away. As Larissa continued to look to him for answers, Rhys turned to look back outside again.

When one of the diseased broke away from the group, Rhys' heart damn near stopped. With its clumsy gait, it shuffled over toward the control booth. The slap of its foot hit the ground, followed by a drag of what must have been its trailing leg. It had an injury of some sort.

It hadn't spotted Rhys, it would have screamed if it had, but the booth seemed to draw its interest. Although slow, the thing made progress toward Rhys and Larissa.

Rhys did what he could to make himself small. Maybe the smoked glass and what must be poor vision through the monster's bloody eyes would keep them hidden from sight.

Maybe.

Who was he kidding?

With the diseased no more than a few metres away, Rhys shook worse than Larissa.

The monster worked its jaw as if it were in pain. If it even felt pain, that is. The desire to run sat loaded in Rhys' muscles. If he needed to, he'd leave Larissa. He couldn't let her drag him down. He looked back at the diseased and saw a bloody mess where its right ear should have been, not that it seemed to care or notice.

The diseased drew closer. Its foot slapped down and it dragged its back leg behind. Another slap of its foot and then a wet *shush* of its trailing leg. A slap of its front foot and a wet *shush*. A slap ... then nothing as the thing stopped a few metres before it reached the booth.

It swayed where it stood and stared straight at Rhys. A tilt of its head to one side and it opened its mouth wide.

Rhys' insides shrivelled and he pulled his knees tighter into his chest. He'd come so far surely it couldn't end now.

Chapter Four

Seventeen months and two weeks ago

Vicky got off the tube at Leicester Square. Some commuters still remained in London, but at eight o'clock in the evening, most of them had gone home for the day.

Good job really; she didn't need to be stuck on a packed and sweaty train in her dinner dress. Not a good first impression to turn up and smell of someone else's body odour.

The ticket barrier opened for Vicky with a *whoosh* as she approached it. As long as she kept her pre-payment card somewhere on her person, the gates would recognise it. A green laser did a quick scan of her. It confirmed her profile matched her card by displaying a green tick while it made a loud *ting*. The gates remained open.

When she looked to her right, she caught sight of her reflection in the large black screens that usually ran adverts. Her flat shoes killed the look and did nothing for her legs, but Brendan had been very specific about her footwear. He'd been so specific in fact, that he freaked her out a little bit. The guy sounded like he had some kind of fetish. He assured her he had a good reason and she'd find out what it was when she got there. At least her practical footwear made the stairs easier to navigate.

Deep breaths failed to settle her pulse as she neared the station's exit. She slowed her pace a little since it wouldn't do to arrive out of breath. It had been a long time since she'd been on a date; she didn't need to fuck it up from the start.

Two weeks had passed since her meltdown in the hospital. What an embarrassment for Brendan to have seen her like that. It would have been different had she actually given a shit about the woman, but after she'd cried in front of him, she felt a strong sense of relief that the old witch had finally gone.

Once at the top of the stairs, Vicky saw Brendan and lost her breath. A gust of warm air crashed into her when she stepped out into the street and stared at the man. Bigger than she remembered him to be, Brendan waited for her in a suit that had been so well tailored it fit him like a second skin. The guy looked like James Bond.

Brendan flashed his pearly white teeth in a broad smile. He walked over and kissed her on each cheek. The subtle yet strong smell of his aftershave suited the man, as she knew him so far. He seemed understated yet incredibly self-assured. She'd never dated anyone like him before.

As Brendan stepped away, he held both of her hands in his own and looked her up and down. He drank her in with his azure assessment before he finally looked back into her eyes, a broad smile on his face.

Vicky's heart pounded and her mouth dried. She pulled her hands away so Brendan didn't feel her sweaty palms.

"I'm *so* glad you came," Brendan said.

"I'll be honest," Vicky replied. "I nearly didn't. I felt so nervous. It's been a long time since I've been out on a date with anyone."

With another warm smile Brendan said, "Sorry to make you wear flat shoes by the way."

"It's fine. I must say I'm intrigued to know why flats are a stipulation though. I'd understand if you were five-foot-two, but I can't imagine many women would make you feel small." Heat smothered Vicky's face. How corny did that sound?

Brendan smiled at her again.

Vicky needed to chill the fuck out. She never went to pieces around men. But then again, she'd never met someone like Brendan before. "So where are we going?" she asked.

Every year it seemed like a newer and taller skyscraper was added to London's skyline. The buildings became more extravagant with each new erection. An architectural pissing contest, it didn't seem like it would end anytime soon. The building of the moment stood in front of them and Brendan pointed at it.

Vicky gasped. "The Umbrella? But it's only been open for three weeks. How did you manage to get a reservation?"

A shrug and Brendan said, "I have contacts." He took one of her hands. "Come on, let's go."

***

The Umbrella, like most of the buildings in London, had been named so due to its appearance. A slim shaft hundreds of metres tall ran all the way up to a restaurant. The restaurant spread out in a huge dome like the top of an umbrella. Although only a nickname, it had stuck. The real name had something to do with the dull corporation that had built the building. Not that Vicky could remember who they were. Not that they would have cared anyway. The restaurant had probably taken enough profit in the first few weeks to pay back their investment and then some. The place took exclusive to a whole new level.

When they arrived at the front of the building, Vicky looked up the long column to the top while Brendan gave his name to a man in a suit. A few seconds later, they were led to a gold-plated door. After the man had pressed his finger against a scanner, the door opened to reveal the building's foyer.

Two lift doors, both gold-plated, stood in the middle of the space. A spiral staircase began on either side of the lifts and wrapped around the back of them. When Vicky tilted her head to look up the glass structure, she saw the staircases made a helix as they twisted around one another all the way to the top. So tall, it made her head spin and the back of her neck ache. Vicky shook her head. "Imagine *walking* up those stairs."

Brendan laughed. "No thanks." He then stepped forward and pressed the call button. The lift pinged and the door on the left opened. Brendan stepped in and Vicky followed him.

Despite the height of the building only two buttons nestled in the gold plated control panel. "Most buildings this tall have so many buttons I go cross-eyed trying to work out which one to press," Vicky said.

"I know, right?"

The top button was engraved with an 'R' and the lower button with a 'G'.

"Restaurant and ground," Brendan said just before he pressed the button for the restaurant.

As the lift rose, the entire thing turned transparent. Clearly made from that fancy colour-changing glass, the projected image vanished and Vicky gasped as they watched the view of London unfold before them. At least it looked like London. It could quite easily be footage of London projected onto a screen.

A pre-recorded message began in a soft female voice from multiple speakers. "Built exclusively for the restaurant at the apex, The Umbrella is the ultimate dining experience. Among the finest restaurants in London, The Umbrella restaurant allows you to have dinner with the gods."

When they reached the halfway point in their assent, Vicky finally remembered to close her open mouth. The recorded voice informed them that the shaft of the building stood at over four hundred metres tall. It accommodated the two lifts, the spiral staircase, and nothing else. Vicky looked up at the restaurant above them and the massive glass dome on top of the shaft. It had a diameter of over one hundred metres. The very outer edges hung down a good fifty metres lower than the point where the restaurant met the shaft. Vicky couldn't even begin to guess how the thing remained upright.

As they continued to go up, Vicky stared out at the city. "This is *amazing*, Brendan."

"Isn't it?" Brendan said. "It's my first time here too."

The conversation died between them but not in an awkward first date kind of way. Vicky found herself mesmerised by the view. She looked across at the tall man next to her; he seemed equally as awestruck.

***

When Vicky looked down, her stomach lurched and she instinctively grabbed onto Brendan. Heat flushed her face when she glanced up and him. "It's going to take some getting used to up here."

After he'd flashed her a warm smile, Brendan held her hand for the remainder of their journey.

***

The tables at the outer edge of the restaurant afforded a full view of the London skyline as well as through the glass floor. The most exclusive tables, Vicky gasped when the maître d' led them over to one.

Glass tables, glass chairs, and a glass floor. When Vicky sat down, she looked at her feet. At four hundred metres from the ground, her stomach lurched again but slightly less this time. She wiggled her feet. "I understand the need for flats now."

Both of them had been given white sock-like covers to slip over their shoes to protect the glass when they walked on it. Brendan smiled. "You can probably see why they limit your alcohol intake. Imagine being pissed *up here*."

***

After they'd ordered, Brendan leaned forward and asked, "So, how are you?"

Heat rushed to Vicky's face and she looked down at her lap. "I'm *so* sorry about the other day. I'm not a crier usually. I don't know what was wrong with me."

"It's fine. You'd just lost someone you lo— someone close to you."

After she'd batted the comment away, Vicky looked back up at him. "Let's not talk about it again. I've grieved for the woman enough. Not that she deserved it. I don't want to give her any more of my time. Why were *you* at the hospital that day?"

For a second or two Brendan stared at Vicky and didn't speak. Tears glazed his eyes and he took a deep breath before he said, "My grandma. She was dying of cancer."

Vicky gasped and clamped her hand to her mouth. "My God. How is she?"

"Dead. She died the same day your mother did. That's why I was in the coffee shop."

"Shit! I'm *sorry*, Brendan. I feel like such a selfish arsehole now."

"It's okay. You needed to grieve at the time. You didn't need my bullshit too."

A shake of her head and Vicky leaned toward Brendan. "Tell me about your grandma."

"She was a good woman. Even when the cancer had her in its grip, she was strong. She had spirit and never backed down. She had a big heart too. If she loved you, she'd do anything for you. My granddad died years ago so she lived by herself for most of my life. I'd visit her every Wednesday for dinner and we'd talk for hours."

"It's Wednesday today," Vicky said.

"Yeah." Brendan smiled. "It felt like the right day to go out. Like it might be a lucky day, you know? A day to celebrate the memory of her."

With her wine glass raised, Vicky said, "To Grandma."

After he'd sipped his drink, Brendan set it down on the table and looked at Vicky. Open sadness in his eyes, he allowed himself to be vulnerable. A flutter ran through Vicky's heart as she watched him.

"She'd be pleased to see me out with a woman like you."

A rush of heat lifted beneath Vicky's skin again. She'd not been this shy since childhood. Brendan had turned her into a giggling schoolgirl. When she realised she needed to respond to his comment, she turned a lock of hair that hung down the side of her face and looked down at the view below again. Before she spoke, she cleared her throat to try and find some composure. "So what do you do for work, Brendan?"

"I work in my dream job. I'm a movie distributor. I get as many free movies as I can watch and I work for all of the big studios. Our company started up a few years back and we managed to provide a better service than anyone else at a fraction of the cost. We got all of the studios on board within the first three years of entering the marketplace, and we're now the market leader." He paused for a second, looked at her and shrugged. "Anyway, that's boring. What do you do?"

"Oh, just an admin job in Summit City … nothing too exciting." Her secrecy contract stipulated that she couldn't talk about work. Rather than admit to being in The Alpha Tower it seemed easier to not tell the whole truth.

"And do you like it?"

"It's a job," Vicky replied.

***

The conversation flowed for the rest of the evening. Brendan talked about his idyllic childhood and his wonderful grandma, and Vicky mostly listened. Brendan kept trying to make her talk, but she didn't need to. To think of her past would have only put a downer on a great evening.

When they stepped out of the lift on the ground floor, the same man who'd let them in let them out again. He and Brendan exchanged the usual formalities as they stepped out into the street.

"Did you enjoy your evening?" the man asked.

Vicky pulled away from their conversation before she could hear Brendan's reply and inhaled a deep lungful of the fresh evening air. A hot summer's night, only the slightest breeze wafted through the city and pressed her light dress against her body.

The night seemed too young but she had to work the next day. Also, she'd managed to get to this point without making too much of a fool of herself. Better to quit while she was ahead.

When Brendan walked over to her, Vicky rubbed the top of his muscular arm. "Thank you for such a *wonderful* evening. It's been a while since I've been on a date, and *never* a date like that." She then leaned forward and kissed him on both cheeks. He smelled as good now as he had before the meal. She could get used to his scent. "Thank you."

Brendan dipped her a nod. "Please let me pay for your taxi home."

Vicky cocked an eyebrow at him.

"I don't mean to come with you. I'll be going back to mine. I just don't want you to get the tube home tonight."

"But I do it *all* the time."

"Honestly," Brendan said and whistled for a cab, "I *insist*."

The taxi pulled up and Brendan opened the door for Vicky to get in. "So will I see you again?"

When someone got this close to Vicky, she usually pushed them away. Relationships led to pain and she'd felt enough of that to last a lifetime. But something about the way Brendan looked at her … his sharp blue eyes and warm smile. The way he treated her … Vicky smiled back at him. "You have my number."

Another nod and Brendan stepped back. "That I do." He then closed the door and banged on the roof of the cab with two heavy thuds.

As Vicky drove away, she watched the tall man stand on the edge of the pavement. Nervous excitement ran butterflies through her stomach. If she allowed herself to fall for him, it would be harder than she'd ever fallen in her life.

Chapter Five

Close to vomiting, Rhys stared at the thing and the thing stared back with its detached crimson glare. It didn't scream like he'd expected it to. Instead, it looked to be in perpetual pain as its face twisted into a constantly shifting grimace. It obviously hadn't seen him. Rhys swallowed but it only served to make him feel more nauseated from the tacky paste that sat at the top of his throat; he hadn't had water in a while.

A quick scan of the booth and Rhys' eyes stopped on the stool. Not a great weapon but better than nothing if he had to fight a pack of the fuckers.

Before the diseased came any closer, a loud explosion sounded out that shook both the fogged up Perspex windows in the booth and the ground Rhys currently sat on. It came from the direction of Summit City.

The monster turned to look across the river, and Rhys watched the thing, desperate for it to move on.

Before it could turn back around and face Rhys, the call of the other diseased rang out in the still evening air. The one by the booth responded with its own yell. It was the first time Rhys had been this close to one while he still remained hidden. He watched as it stumbled off to join the others.

A shake ran through Rhys and he released a heavy sigh. The dirty Perspex windows must have been filthy enough to hide them and save their lives; that and the handicap of what must have been poor vision through its bleeding eyes.

Several more explosions ran through the cold concrete ground like a line of gigantic fire crackers had gone off. "That must have been a car park."

When Rhys looked down to see Larissa stare up at him through bloodshot eyes, he added, "It sounded like a collection of cars exploding."

Another exhalation, so hard it puffed his cheeks out, and Rhys leaned his head against the hard wall behind him. "Thank fuck!"

***

After a minute or two, Rhys sat up higher so he could see out of the booth. He could feel Larissa's eyes on him as he watched the events outside. "They're all gathered over by the river's edge. All seven of the fuckers. They must like bright lights and loud noises. I think we should make our move now."

"But there are seven of them out there, Rhys."

"Better than ten."

"Yeah, but *seven*! We *can't* fight our way past seven of them."

Rhys filled his lungs with the booth's stale air. It did little to calm him down and worsened the dry funky taste in his mouth. Reminiscent of the last fast food burger he'd eaten, he ran his tongue beneath his top row of teeth to try to banish the flat taste.

The action proved ineffective. After a quick scan of the booth, he sighed. "We'll have to use the stool."

"What the fuck are we going to do with a stool? Sit on it and tell jokes to them? Are you fucking *mental*, Rhys?"

The chrome frame, although spindly, looked like it could do some damage. "It'll have to do. Hopefully they won't see us. Let me carry it first, and then when we're out of the way of the diseased, we can break it up and use the legs as weapons." Larissa opened her mouth but Rhys cut her off. "You got a better idea?"

After a slight pause, Larissa shook her head and dropped her eyes to the ground.

"Right, let's do this then."

***

To stand up seemed like insanity. So vulnerable in the booth and now entirely visible, Rhys watched Larissa slowly get to her feet too. "Hurry up, will ya?"

She looked in pain from the time spent on the hard ground. "I'm going as quickly as I can."

A glance through the fogged windows and Rhys watched the pack of diseased. "Well, it ain't quick enough. There's only so long those things can stare at the burning city before they get bored. I'd like to be long gone by the time that happens."

When Larissa finally stood up, Rhys held his breath as he pushed the booth's door open. It yawned a gentle creak. Each pop of the dry hinges twisted Rhys' anxiety tighter. He looked across at the diseased, but none of them seemed to notice them.

While he bit down on his bottom lip, Rhys pushed the door wide open in one quick movement. He let Larissa out before him. After he'd taken the stool, he stepped out with her.

The reek of the diseased hung heavier than ever. The strong shot of rot lifted Rhys' tongue to the roof of his mouth. With the stool in one of his hands, Rhys pointed over in the direction the diseased had come from.

Larissa looked to where he'd pointed and back at him before she mouthed the word 'really?'

Rhys nodded and led the way.

Rhys' legs turned to jelly as they walked. In the huge open space the only cover they had sat on the road in the lone form of the abandoned police car. The diseased stood behind a small wall as they watched the city burn. Clumsy with fear, Rhys stumbled. He managed to regain his balance and snap the stool back just before it clattered against the ground. His heart beat in his neck as he looked at the diseased, who seemed oblivious to what had just happened, and then Larissa, who reflected his own panic back at him through her wide eyes and open mouth.

He looked away from her and took several breaths to calm his nerves. The smell of burned plastic rode on the back of the diseased's vinegar rot. Rhys set off again.

The pair of them walked on tiptoes as they crossed the space behind the diseased. Rhys glanced down at Oscar's axe when they passed the police car. He could pick it up. An axe would do a world of damage compared to a stupid stool, but something about it didn't sit right. Whenever he used the weapon, he'd think about the psychopath currently on the tail of Vicky and his child.

Rhys' pulse beat so hard it upset his balance, but he pushed on.

Once past the police car they had nowhere else to hide. He picked up his pace and Larissa followed.

About twenty metres from the brow of the hill the diseased screamed. Their phlegmy cry snapped Rhys' body tight and he turned to look at them.

But they hadn't seen him. Because of the low sun, Rhys had to squint across the river to see the reason for their excitement.

A woman, or at least it seemed like a woman, Rhys found it hard to tell from the distance that separated them, ran from the burning city. Fuck knows how she managed to avoid the flames. If she could find a boat maybe she'd get out of there.

The diseased screamed across the river at her and they became more agitated as she ran.

Then Rhys looked behind her and a cold chill snapped through him. A horde of about twenty of the fuckers, some of them on fire from the incineration, chased on her tail. Arms out in front of them and jaws spread wide, they bellowed insane fury as they followed her.

A pang of regret twisted through Rhys' chest. If he could have helped the woman, he would have, but he couldn't do anything from the other side of the river. To react would be to give him and Larissa away and would do fuck all to help her. He turned to Larissa and saw her watching the chaos in Summit City. When she looked at him, he pointed at the brow of the hill. "Come on, let's get the fuck out of here."

***

On the other side of the hill, Larissa turned to Rhys and spoke in a whisper. "Do you think she made it?"

"Probably not."

"That's nice!"

"Well, what do you expect? I don't think she made it. What were the odds? She had a rugby team of diseased on her tail and looked like she didn't have a clue where to go to get off the island."

After a deep sigh, Larissa turned to him again. "Where are *we* going?"

"North."

"Very specific."

"We're going to head in the direction of Flynn's school and then into central London. We need to get through the city to get to The Highlands. That was where Vicky wanted to go."

Larissa threw her arms up in exasperation. "And you think we can trust *that,* do you? I'd stop thinking about what Vicky would do and come up with a better plan."

When Rhys stopped dead, Larissa did the same and looked at him. "Look," he said, "if you have any *better* ideas, I'd love to hear them. If all you're going to do is bitch and moan then keep it to yourself, yeah? I'm getting bored of listening to your whining voice. I've rescued you from the city now and I can't continue to be responsible for you. You wanna go in a different direction, *fine*, you do that. Jog on, love. You wanna come with me? Then shut the fuck up."

Before Larissa had a chance to reply, Rhys set off again. Seconds later, he heard the slap of her socked feet run up the road after him.

Chapter Six

About six months ago

Vicky hadn't used an underground train for months because of the terrorist attacks. But she couldn't live in fear of the lunatics who identified with the East's cause. If they took her freedom away they'd won, and she wouldn't let that happen.

The train journey had passed without incident, but the sheer weight of people on the hot summer's evening made it hard for her to breathe as she navigated the tube station to get to the exit. With every step forward, she either knocked into someone or someone knocked into her. So cramped she had to pull her elbows to her side and every surge in the throng threatened to throw her to the ground. With the reek of body odour and halitosis around her, Vicky focused on the fresh air that waited for her out in the street.

As she pushed and shoved, the sound of hundreds of people in the enclosed space sent her mind into a spin. Dizzy with panic, she looked over the heads of the crowd. With the exit in sight, she only had to hold it together for a few more metres at most. *But what if a bomb went off now?*

By the time she'd stepped on the first step that lead out of the station, her heart hammered and her throat had dried to the point where she could taste the stale air around her. Her accelerated pulse sent her head into a spin and her legs shook like they could give way beneath her at any moment. Nausea turned over in her stomach.

Once at the top of the stairs, she fell out into the cooler evening air and filled her lungs. A shake still ran through her and she had to wipe her sweaty palms against her jeans, but she'd made it.

The fear had been with her since the day she'd narrowly avoided death about a year ago. Maybe it would never vanish. Therapy, self-help books, and advice from friends didn't help to still the panic that flapped in her chest like a trapped bird. *Face the fear and do it anyway. Like fuck!* She faced the fear and the next day she had to face the fear all over again. No more diluted from repetition, she faced it again and again and again.

Another deep breath and she exhaled hard as if to force the anxiety from her body. Brendan didn't need a stressed out fiancée at this meal. But she'd had a rough day and the journey hadn't helped one bit. She focused on her feet to try to ground her panic.

When she looked through the crowd, she saw Brendan by the door to the restaurant. They ate there every Wednesday. 'Grandma Day' they called it. Not one for traditions usually, even Vicky felt the importance of Grandma Day. Without a Wednesday meal with Grandma, Brendan had been lost. What better way to celebrate one of the most important women in his life than to eat a meal out with *the* most important woman in his life, his words, not Vicky's.

Vicky stood on tiptoes and waved when Brendan looked over. She then checked the street for cars and crossed the road.

Brendan held the door open for her like he always did, and they entered the restaurant together.

As always, the table in the corner had their silver 'reserved' sign on it. No matter how busy The Jade Garden got, Vicky and Brendan always had the same table reserved for them on a Wednesday night.

Vicky made eye contact with the waitress, Sandy—a name she'd chosen to save the customers embarrassment when they couldn't pronounce her native Chinese name, who nodded at her. Vicky walked over to her table with Brendan behind her, the air in the busy restaurant alive with chattering voices and the chink of cutlery against porcelain plates. In spite of all the terrorist activity, The Jade Garden never suffered for business. It helped that they flew The Union Jack out the front of their restaurant and were always the first to speak out against any acts of violence aimed at the West.

When they sat down by the window, Vicky let some of the tension slide from her body and smiled at the man she loved. "It's *good* to see you."

"And on our anniversary," Brendan said. "I know it's not a full year until tomorrow, but it seemed appropriate to celebrate it today."

As Vicky looked at her love, calmness spread through her. Despite what she'd found out that day, everything would be all right as long as they were together.

"We could have gone anywhere to eat, you know?" Brendan said. "I think it's the eating out part that's important for a Wednesday, not where we do it."

A shrug and Vicky pushed a shot of air through her lips as if to dismiss his concern. "It seems right to spend it in the same place we spend every other Grandma Day." Because some of the tension had eased from her stomach, Vicky drew a lungful of the restaurant's air. The smell of fried rice and the sweet Chinese sauces made her mouth water.

When Sandy came over with a bottle of Champagne, Brendan placed his palm across his heart and offered the waitress a warm smile. For such an imposing man he wore his emotions with pride. Unafraid to show he cared, his entire face lit up at the gesture.

"Happy anniversary," she said, her Chinese accent as strong now as it had been a year ago when they'd started visiting the place.

Brendan dipped a nod at her. "Thank you, Sandy, we really appreciate it."

After Sandy had filled both glasses, Brendan looked over at Marcus, the owner of the restaurant, and raised his drink.

Marcus returned a warm smile and gentle nod.

"Would you like the usual?" Sandy asked.

Brendan laughed. "I always want to say no, but what I have is *so* good that I don't *want* to try anything else. Vick?"

Although she'd relaxed, Vicky still didn't fire on all cylinders. What she'd discovered that day had rocked her world and she still reeled from it. She took a second to find her bearings before she forced a smile at Sandy. "I'll have the usual too, please."

Sandy bowed at them and walked away.

With her glass still aloft, Vicky smiled at Brendan and started the meal in the same way they started every Wednesday meal. "To Grandma."

"To Grandma," Brendan replied.

The Champagne fizzed on Vicky's tongue and she swallowed the sharp drink. Before she'd put the glass down, Brendan reached across the table and held her hand. "What's wrong?"

"What? Nothing's wrong." Not that she could hide it from Brendan.

A raised eyebrow and Brendan remained silent.

Vicky looked at the table. "I dunno. I suppose the train journey just stressed me out today. With it being nearly a year ago since the attack and all. If you hadn't insisted I'd taken a cab on that night, I would have been on that train."

The warmth of Brendan's strong grip squeezed her hand and Vicky continued. "I just can't help but think about those poor people on the underground. Not a single one of them survived. I avoided death that day. I shouldn't be here now."

"If you should have been one of them you *would* have been. I know it's hard to see, but *everything* happens for a reason, and there's a reason you're still here. You have something *amazing* to offer this world."

She laughed. "As the building manager for," she lowered her voice, "The Alpha Tower?" When in a place where anyone could hear the conversation it made sense to keep her voice down. Not that she had much power in her job, but with the secrecy contracts she'd had to sign it made life easier to hide where she worked.

Another squeeze of her hand and Brendan said, "Don't play yourself down, darling. You have a lot to offer the world. You're one of life's good eggs."

Tears stung Vicky's eyes. She blinked repeatedly and fanned her face with her hand. "Don't be kind to me."

Whenever they held hands, Brendan always stroked the rock on Vicky's finger. After only six months of knowing her, he'd proposed and she'd said yes. The way he caressed the jewel seemed to show his pride for what it meant rather than the material value of the object. She was his future wife, the most important person in his world. "We need to thank the gods that you didn't get on that train though." He laughed. "It's almost like I knew the attack was going to happen."

A cold chill snapped through Vicky as if struck by a cool breeze. "I had my doubts about a second date, you know. But after that, I knew I couldn't let you go. I'd found my guardian angel."

Brendan glowed and straightened in his seat.

Vicky then sighed. "The journey here was tough. I suppose it doesn't help when the terrorist attacks continue and no one has been caught for them. Anything could be wired to blow." After she'd looked around the restaurant at all the other diners, Vicky looked back at Brendan. "Anyone could be a terrorist. There could be one in here right *now* and we'd be none the wiser."

Brendan's shoulders shook when he laughed. "There *aren't* any terrorists in here."

"How do you know?"

He laughed again before his face turned serious. "But that

isn't it, Vick. I know you. We've talked about the terrorist attack plenty since it happened. What's going on? Something's happened *today*."

"How do you do it?"

Brendan shrugged. "Do what?"

With her attention directed down at the table again, Vicky ran circles on the top of it with her finger. "See straight through me. How do you do it?" Before Brendan could reply, Vicky continued. "I found something out at work today … I kind of suspected wrong doings, but nothing on this level. I found out what they do on the top floor of the tower. It's not fucking good, Brendan."

"It's okay if you don't want to talk about it. I understand. I'm here if you need someone to listen, but I don't want you to feel like you need to break your secrecy contract."

Tears stung Vicky's eyes and her vision blurred. "I *want* to tell you more than anything, but—"

Brendan stroked her forearm. "It's okay. *Honestly*, it's fine. I understand."

A shake took a hold of Vicky and her hands trembled as she picked at the loose skin along the side of her thumb. "I want to tell you more than anything, really I do. Shit's going to hit the fan in a few months, but I don't think there's anything I can do about it."

When Brendan said nothing, Vicky lifted her glass of Champagne, took a huge gulp, and stared past him out of the window. "I feel so fucking powerless."

Chapter Seven

"Come *on*," Rhys said as he pulled on Larissa's hand for what felt like the hundredth time. He held two of the stool legs in his other hand. Once they'd gotten far enough away from the police car and the diseased, Rhys had stopped and pulled the stool apart. Four spears, sharp from where they'd been ripped from the stool, he'd kept two for himself and had given two to Larissa. "We need to run. We need to catch up with them."

The cycle repeated again as Larissa tried to run for about ten metres before she stopped. "I *can't*. It hurts my feet too much. I need shoes before I can even think about running. If we keep this up for much longer I'll probably step on something and won't even be able to walk."

Although Rhys slowed down, he kept the pace brisk. He looked at the woodland area that ran along the side of the wide seven-lane highway, fourteen lanes if you counted the other side of the road. Packed so dense with trees, the area could contain a horde of diseased and they wouldn't know until the fuckers sprung them. He'd stared into the darkness so many times he started to see movement where there wasn't any.

About fifteen minutes had passed since they'd left the diseased back at the bloody police car. The summer solstice had happened just a few days ago, so despite it being nearly ten o'clock at night the sun still ran a slight tint through the sky. The air had turned to the grey half-light of dusk and the temperature had dropped.

A glance back toward Summit City and Rhys watched the orange glow on the horizon. They may have been farther away, but it glowed brighter because of the rapidly diminishing light. The molten rubber reek hung as heavy as ever.

"I still can't believe the city has fallen," Rhys said. A scan for Building Seventy-two and he laughed. "I could never pick our building out on the skyline before, but I definitely can't now. At least we'll never have to go back to that horrible place again. I hope the city burns for a long time. It seems to be pulling the diseased toward it."

Larissa looked around. "It's weird how quiet it is. Especially considering how crazy the city was."

"You know what I think?" Rhys said.

Larissa didn't respond.

"I think the disease didn't spread very far from the city. I think a handful got out and Vicky and I saw the worst of it at Flynn's school. But I reckon they've been pulled back in. Maybe attracted to the bright flames on the horizon. There's only one town and a school within a mile radius of Summit City so there can't have been that many people to infect. I think we'll be able to outrun this and get through London before it falls."

Larissa still didn't reply to Rhys as a dark frown spread across her face. The mention of Vicky seemed to have soured her already bad mood. Not that Rhys could blame her for her state of mind as things were hardly fucking rosy.

Rhys stopped in the road and turned to Larissa. Around the next bend were the executed police officers he and Vicky had seen. It served as the first sign for him that the virus was more than an accident. Not wanting to mention Vicky again, Rhys said, "You need to be ready for what you're about to see."

After she'd raised an eyebrow at him, Larissa sighed. "I've seen children biting the throats out of old women today, Rhys. I think I can cope with whatever's around this corner."

She had a point. After he'd dipped a sharp nod at her Rhys said, "Fine." He then raised his two stool legs so he had one in each hand. Spears more than bludgeons, they'd have to do. "I'm hoping there won't be anything to fight around this corner, but it won't do any harm to have them ready anyway."

Larissa's green eyes narrowed and she raised her spears too.

***

When they rounded the corner the heavy tang of piss and shit hit them square on. Rhys pressed the back of his hand into his nose as he stumbled backward.

He gagged and his eyes watered as he took in the sight.

Next to him, Larissa stood and watched the scene with cold detachment. The wind had picked up and it tossed her black bobbed hair.

"It's looks different from when Vicky and I saw it."

"Different?"

The images were so stark Rhys squinted as he stared at them. "The police …" He looked at a policewoman close to them. A bullet hole in her head, she also had a huge chunk torn from her stomach.

"It looks like something's tried to eat her," Larissa said. "Isn't that what they do?"

"It wasn't like this when we saw them earlier. And *no*, they don't do that. They bite. They infect. But it seems that once you're infected they leave you alone. This is them …" the word stuck in his throat and his entire being sank "… *feeding*. They've been feeding. I hate to think what we would have found here had the fire not pulled all of the diseased toward the city. It looks like it interrupted some kind of fucked up banquet."

Only one police car remained at the scene and it now sat as a charred wreck. The road surface around it had turned black from the flames. "Fuck it."

Larissa looked at Rhys.

"I was hoping we'd find some better means of transport. Vicky sounded like she was running with Flynn, so a car would have caught us up to them much quicker."

Larissa didn't respond as she stared at the policewoman on the ground.

The pair moved off again and it took all of Rhys' will to not look down at the half-eaten woman. He had enough nightmares queued up in his head already, he didn't need any more.

Rhys may have avoided a glance at the police officer, but he looked at Larissa to see she hadn't taken her eyes off her.

When she got next to her, Larissa stopped and sat on the road.

"What the fuck are you doing?" Rhys said.

But Larissa didn't reply. Instead, she pressed the soles of her feet up against the soles of the police officer's shoes.

The penny suddenly dropped for Rhys. "Are they your size?"

Larissa chewed the inside of her mouth and frowned as she eyed up the shoes. "They'll do."

Rhys squatted down next to Larissa and his knees burned from the movement. He could have stayed on his feet, but they needed to move on, and if he helped her, they could get going quicker.

Although a few feet away from the mauled part of her body, Rhys still shook as he touched the woman. What if she reanimated? Then he looked at the bullet hole that had killed her. It may have been small at the front, but a huge pool of blood swelled behind her head. She wasn't getting up from that. Sweat turned Rhys' palms damp as he pulled at the laces. He slipped the shoe free and passed it to Larissa.

While Larissa put the shoes on, Rhys said, "We can run quicker than Flynn, and Oscar's injured so I don't see him moving too fast. Hopefully we can catch up to them if we increase our pace."

Although she didn't look up, Larissa still said, "If we're heading in the right direction, that is."

"I think we are."

"But how can you know that, Rhys? She could have taken him anywhere."

"Yeah, she could, but I think she's headed to The Highlands like she said she would. To do that, she'd have to go through London. We need to take the quickest route to London. I think if we're fast, we can get ahead of the virus and get out of the city before it becomes overrun."

"It's nice to have a plan, Rhys, but I still doubt your logic. She could be going *anywhere*. We're just pissing in the wind by trying to follow her. Is this another time where we have to have"—she made air quotes— "'faith'? We need to trust in the *force* or something? We need to behave like we're some kind of Jedi masters and follow our hearts on a wild fucking goose chase?"

Tired of her bullshit, Rhys sighed. "And you have a better idea, do you? Or do you just want to spend this entire time criticising me for taking some kind of action?"

After she'd tied her other shoe, Larissa got to her feet and looked up the road in the direction they needed to head. She clearly didn't have a better solution, so she said, "Come on, let's get out of here. I don't like seeing this crap."

Not an apology, far fucking from it in fact, but it would have to do.

***

For the next ten minutes or so, the pair ran. The slap of their shoes against the hard road existed as the only sound between them. The aches of the past day caught up with Rhys again and the hard jolts of his feet against the road ran shocks up his back. It twisted the ache at the bottom of his spine from the bike crash.

In the half-mind of running, most of his attention on his breaths, Rhys couldn't police his thoughts like he could when he walked. Sadness turned his limbs heavy and the tightness in his throat made it hurt to breathe. He spoke between gasps for air. "I can't … believe … Dave's gone."

For the first time since they'd found the bloody police car Larissa's cold demeanour warmed a little. A sympathetic frown furrowed her brow. She first looked at the woodland area that ran alongside the road before she said, "It's sad. I'm sorry for your loss, Rhys."

"And you yours. I know how much Clive meant to you."

A sharp nod and Larissa looked in front of her again. Their footsteps synchronised and they pushed on.

The woodland area on their right pulled away when they arrived at the first town. They slowed to a fast walk as they took the place in. Rhys' eyes stung from where sweat had run into them and a shimmer ran through his heart. "This was when I realised the virus had gotten out of the city. Vicky and I came through here and saw blood on the streets." As the first garage door came into view Rhys said, "It was that garage—" He couldn't finish the sentence.

In big red letters in what could have only been blood, read, 'R - Call Me - 07734 921118 - V.'

Despite his exhaustion and jagged fear, Rhys smiled. "I told you we should head this way. I knew we'd be on the right track if we did."

"Do you have a phone?"

Rhys' frame sagged. "No. Do you?"

A shake of her head and Larissa sighed. "We need to get that number down and find one."

Rhys chewed on his bottom lip as he looked around for something. He then clicked his fingers when he saw a large bush to his right. "I've got it." Rhys walked over to it and pulled ten of its long and waxy green leaves off.

"What are you doing?" Larissa said.

"Ten leaves. I'll tear slits into them for each number and stack them in the correct order."

"But there's *eleven* numbers."

"I think I'll remember the first number's a zero."

Larissa didn't reply.

Night had well and truly settled in by the time Rhys had finished. He slipped the stacked leaves into his pocket in order. "Right," he said, "all we need now is a phone."

Dark as it was outside, every window on every house looked even darker. Not a single light had been switched on in the street. Maybe a power cut, maybe just a sign of an abandoned town. Whatever the reason, Rhys' body wound tight as he stood in the near silence of the place.

With Larissa by his side, Rhys walked over to the first house. "If only it were like the old days when people actually had a landline."

As Larissa walked next to him she said, "I don't fucking like it here. There could be anything in any of these houses."

"Don't worry; I think the town cleared out a while ago." The warble in his voice undermined his confidence, but Larissa didn't pull him up on it.

Rhys approached the first house in the street, the one with the bloody garage door. He walked up to a dark window and only saw his reflection. When he stepped closer still, his warm breath turned to condensation on the glass. It made it harder to see inside.

With his hands cupped around either side of his face to block out even the moonlight, Rhys pressed against the window and stared into the dark room. His skin tingled as adrenaline surged through him. It looked like the living room from what he could see. It seemed empty. "I'm not sure we're going to have much—"

The face of a diseased sprung up on the other side of the pane and Rhys' heart damn near jumped from his chest. A huge chunk of flesh hung from the side of its face like a rancid strip of steak. With hatred locked onto Rhys through its bloody eyes, it opened its mouth and released its war cry.

Chapter Eight

About twenty-two weeks ago

"Look, Vicky," Brendan said as he pulled a chair out and sat down at the kitchen table opposite her, "it's been over two weeks since our anniversary meal and"—he reached over and held both of her hands—"I'm not prying, but you've been different. Whatever you found out at work that day is eating you up, and I want to help if I can."

Vicky looked out the window to her right. The entire wall on that side of their penthouse apartment was made from glass. The tallest building for a few miles around, it gave them a great view. London sat as a backdrop with the towered skyline an ever-changing sight of architectural competition. Phallus after phallus, each one grander and bigger than the one next to it. *And who said it was a man's world?*

In the foreground, however, stood the Alpha Tower. The sight of it hadn't bothered Vicky when they moved in. To see it every time she looked out of the window now made the knot in her stomach twist tighter. Although the tower hadn't bothered her at first, she wouldn't have chosen the flat, but Brendan loved the view. He said it was perfect. And seeing as he'd been the one paying for it, it made sense that Vicky should honour his wishes. But now *everything* had changed.

When she looked back at him, Brendan shrugged. "So, do you want to talk about it?"

"Of course I want to talk about it." Vicky ground her jaw and her vision blurred. She swallowed against the burn in her throat. "I want to talk about it more than ever. But I *can't*. I'm sworn to secrecy, remember?"

A frown creased Brendan's forehead. "But you can trust me, Vic."

Some of the tension left Vicky as the grief took over. It rushed through her as a hot wave and her eyes watered. A deep and stuttered sigh and she said, "I know I can. I know."

Brendan squeezed her hands. "Look, I wouldn't normally pry, but I'm worried about you. Whatever it is you're keeping to yourself is clearly eating you up. I can help if you let me."

If she continued to look into his intense blue stare, she'd give everything away, so Vicky looked down at the glass-topped table. For a few seconds she focused on one spot in front of her and felt her breaths; in and out, in and out. When things overwhelmed her, she tried to bring herself into the present moment. Nothing mattered but the now. It made no sense to try to think beyond that point. When she thought of the future, she couldn't see a way out.

When she looked back up warm tears rolled down her cheeks. Another deep and stuttered breath and she said, "I found out what they do in the Alpha Tower."

Brendan straightened his back and leaned toward her. "What is it? You can tell me."

He sounded keen, not a surprise really. If she'd lived with him like this for the past few weeks, she'd be champing at the bit to find out what was up his arse. "*Zombies*, Brendan."

Brendan jumped back and his seat screeched over the hard floor. "*Zombies?*"

"I know. It sounds fucking *mental*, doesn't it?"

"What do you mean *zombies*? You'll have to give me a little more than that."

Unable to control the shake that ran through her, Vicky pulled her hand away from Brendan and bit one of her fingernails. It had been years since she'd bitten them and she could still smell the lemon hand wash she'd used earlier that day. "We have the whole weapons embargo, right?"

"Yep," Brendan said.

"And we're stuck in the middle of this stupid cold war."

"And may that end as soon as possible."

"Well, I think they've moved into bio-weapons."

"And they're making them in the Alpha Tower?" Brendan asked.

"Exactly."

"But how do you know?"

"Artem."

"Your ex-boyfriend?"

"Yep. He showed me some CCTV footage from the labs. He works in building management too, but in the control room. He's known for some time. He's sworn to secrecy but he had to show somebody else."

"And you *saw* a zombie?"

"Well no, but—"

"How do you know they're making a virus then?"

"We heard a couple of scientists talk about it. About how the disease was coming along, about how it would put an end to this civil war. About how it would tear through The East until there was no one left."

What looked like fury but must have been something else, discomfort or maybe revulsion, gripped a hold of Brendan's features and his warm hands left Vicky's as he withdrew. Then as quickly as it had settled on him, it vanished.

"Sorry," Brendan said and shook his head and reached across for her hands again. "That was a bit of a shock to hear."

"I know, right? That's why I've been so messed up about it. Now don't get me wrong, I don't like The East."

"Who does?"

"But I don't want to see a virus dropped on it either. Just because our leaders can't get along it doesn't mean their children should die, their schoolteachers, their doctors …" her voice trailed off.

Brendan shook his head and looked out of the window at the city. After a few seconds, he turned back to Vicky. "You've *got* to leave."

"I want to, more than anything,"—exhaustion tugged on Vicky's frame—"but I *can't*. If I leave, they'll *know* something's up. I told them everything was great a few weeks ago. How would that look if I suddenly decided I didn't want to work there anymore? They wouldn't risk it. They'd make me …" She choked on her words before she finally said, "They'd make me disappear."

The screech of Brendan's chair pulled Vicky's shoulders up to her neck. He got to his feet, walked around the table, and hugged her. His aftershave, strong yet subtle, offered a familiar comfort. She leaned against his well-developed chest and felt the vibration of his deep voice along the side of her face.

"Shit Vic, I see what you mean. You're right. You need to stay. But what's happening there is *horrible*. Completely unforgivable. We'll figure something out, okay?"

Both blinded and choked by her tears Vicky sobbed as she nodded. When Brendan squeezed her harder she said, "I love you."

"I love you too, honey, and don't worry. We'll get through this."

Chapter Nine

The *crash* of the breaking window called out into the night air as the diseased leaped through it at Rhys.

With his arms out in front of him, he deflected the thing without getting bitten. Two *chings* sounded out as he dropped both of his stool legs, and a sharp pain ran through his shoulder blades when he fell onto the hard driveway.

The smell of decay overwhelmed him as he sat up and stared at the hideous creature. He scrambled backwards, his tired legs sluggish from the day's exertion. A mixture of adrenaline, exhaustion, and pain spun through his head, but he kept moving.

The diseased hopped up into an animalistic crouch, stared at Rhys though its bloody eyes, and roared again before it charged at him.

Because Rhys hadn't gotten to his feet, he fell flat on his back again as the thing jumped on top of him.

Sandwiched between the monster and the hard concrete driveway, Rhys reached up and grabbed the diseased around its throat. Its cold, clammy, and wax-like skin sent gooseflesh down both of Rhys' arms. Rhys shook beneath its weight as he watched the angry thing bite at the air between them. A series of castanet clicks snapped near his face, but none of them connected. The thing only had half of its teeth left in its dark mouth.

Rhys' knuckles ached as he tightened his grip. It felt like trying to choke a constrictor.

The monster twisted and writhed as if to break free of Rhys' grasp. When it turned to the side Rhys saw the gash down the side of its face. At about six inches, long the tacky wound bore the evidence of where it had been bitten.

With his teeth clenched, Rhys growled and pushed against his own shaking arms to keep the monster away from him. But the thing started to overpower him and his flagging strength was no match for the beast's weight and desire.

As the monster pushed down, Rhys had to turn his head to avoid its bloody drool. Warm and tacky, it landed against his neck like snot. The pungent reek of rot made Rhys' eyes water while the hard driveway burned his shoulder blades.

Rhys closed his eyes as he dug deep and he screamed through his clenched teeth as his entire body shook. He couldn't hold out much longer. Then the pressure suddenly eased. He looked up to see one of the stool legs driven through the side of the thing's face. The pole had been rammed so hard it had gone straight through the diseased's head and out the other side.

The monster fell off him and Larissa followed up with her other stool leg. Wild-eyed and red faced, she stabbed the creature repeatedly in the side of its head.

Rhys got to his feet, rolled the pain from his shoulders, and watched her pepper the thing with stab wounds. Its bloody right eye had popped from its head and rested on the driveway. A stringy line of nerves and muscles led back into the dark red socket.

"I think you've done enough," Rhys said.

Larissa stabbed it four more times before she finally eased up. Sweat beaded her brow and she drew heavy breaths. "I wanted to make sure."

Another glance down at the pulped mess on the driveway and Rhys laughed. "I think you've done that." He shrugged and offered her a tight-lipped smile. "That was close."

Before Larissa could reply, the scream of more diseased sounded out behind them.

Rhys grabbed the two stool legs he'd dropped earlier and Larissa removed her second one from the side of the creature's head.

At first, they heard the patter of feet as it came around the side of the house. Seconds later, four more diseased appeared. Arms out in front of them, they sprinted with their usual clumsiness. Appearing as if on the verge of a fall, they ran with a forward tilt but, as always, remained on their feet.

Although smarter than the movie zombies, when the diseased sensed prey, they didn't seem able to do anything but attack. They continued toward Rhys and Larissa at a flat-out sprint.

Rhys picked the one at the front. He used the creature's momentum against it and speared it in the centre of its face. The stool leg passed straight through it and out of the other side with a wet *squelch*. Rhys let go of his weapon and evaded the charging monster. It stumbled past him for several more steps before it fell to the ground, the pressure of the impact driving the stool leg all the way through its head. When he glanced at Larissa, he saw she'd done the same with another one of the four.

Rhys and Larissa took another diseased each. Slower than the first two, the second pair seemed to approach with a modicum of caution.

The one that focused on Rhys snapped at the air between them. Its teeth clicked and it released a phlegmy death rattle before it lunged forward.

Although not as thick as his baseball bat, Rhys swung for the diseased with the stool leg anyway. The *ting* of the thin, hollow pole rang out and a vibration ran all the way down to his tight grip. It dazed the thing and nothing more.

Rhys didn't give it a chance to recover. He swung for it again and again. With his teeth clenched, he swung and swung. Each hit struck on or around the creature's temple.

After several heavy swings, Rhys' hands tingled from the vibrations. The monster swayed, clearly dazed by the attack.

Rhys seized his moment. With both hands on the stool leg, he lunged the sharp end forward into the diseased's eye. A shot of rancid air belched from the fresh hole.

After he'd jumped aside Rhys watched the monster fall to the ground face first. Like the other one he'd just killed, the crash landing drove the pole farther into its head as it lay limp and lifeless.

When he looked across at Larissa, he watched her lose it on the fourth and final diseased as she drove jab after jab after jab into its bloody face.

"Larissa," Rhys said.

She continued to stab the thing.

"Larissa."

Jab, jab, jab.

Rhys spoke louder. "Larissa!"

She finally stopped and looked at him. A deep frown crushed her face and she panted from the exertion.

"I think we're done here."

As one, they remained silent and listened. The horrible noise the things made was simultaneously the best and worst thing about them. Every time Rhys heard it, it sent ice through his veins, but at least they announced their arrival. Silence hung in the air.

After a few seconds, Rhys turned back to Larissa. "Thank you for saving me."

A sharp nod and the hatred Larissa had looked at him with since they'd crossed the river seemed to dilute ever so slightly. She almost smiled when she said, "Welcome." Almost.

With a diseased by his feet, Rhys squatted down and rifled through the thing's pockets.

"What are you *doing*?" Larissa asked.

"Looking for a phone."

Larissa then dropped down and searched the two diseased she'd taken out. Rhys saw her pull a lighter from the pocket of one of them. A sturdy Zippo lighter, it clicked when she opened it and sparked when she struck the wheel. The flame seemed strong. She snapped it shut again and slipped it into her pocket.

Rhys checked the last of the five, the one that had jumped through the window to attack him, and he felt the small slab in its pocket. "Ah-ha." He pulled the phone out. The screen had been cracked, but the green battery light on its side remained on. Rhys pressed the home button.

"Fuck it!"

"What?" Larissa asked.

"It's one of the new ones."

"The ones that need breath, voice, and skin scent recognition?"

"Yeah. A corpse won't get you into one of these. You need to be living and breathing to access it. We could be here forever trying to find one of the old ones with just fingerprint access. I mean, who even has those phones anymore?"

Rhys threw the handset to the ground.

Chapter Ten

About sixteen weeks ago

It got worse every day for Vicky. The second the security guards stepped aside to let her into the Alpha Tower, the anxious buzz in her stomach began. By lunchtime, she'd lost her appetite. When she finally got ready to leave each day, her guts writhed like she'd swallowed a bag of snakes. It took until well into the evening before she could climb into bed for another fitful night's sleep.

All day, no matter what task she set her mind to, she could only think about the experiments that went on in the Alpha Tower's penthouse. She watched every person who entered the building and thought about his or her equal over in The East. Innocents didn't deserve to die for the sake of government paranoia.

Before she'd found out about the lab upstairs, she would have stayed late if a job needed to be finished. Not anymore. The second it hit five o'clock, Vicky left work. One day, she even left her computer on in her haste to get out. She got a bollocking the next day for that one. Security risk … blah blah … waste of electricity … blah blah blah.

A swipe of her card through the card reader and she left the Alpha Tower for yet another day. When the main door opened, she felt the fresh summer breeze and filled her lungs with a deep inhale. The sun, magnified by the bright windows in the city, blinded Vicky and she had to squint to see clearly. Her eyes already burned from lack of sleep, so she fished around in her handbag for her sunglasses but couldn't find them. She must have left them at home.

Vicky blinked repeatedly until she finally saw the unmistakable figure walk toward her. Broad and tall, he stood straight and proud. He'd come to meet his woman, and nothing could make him happier. Vicky's heart lifted as she stepped toward him. After a quick glance around to be sure nobody could hear her, she spoke with a lowered voice. "Brendan? What are you doing here?"

"I wanted to meet you from work."

"That's really kind of you, but *how* did you get into the city without a pass?"

After he'd looked at all the people around them, Brendan lowered his voice too. "It's quite easy if you have enough confidence in your blag. Most of the time, I have people apologising to me as they let me in."

"You come here often?"

"Sometimes. It's nice to check it out, you know?"

Before Vicky could reply, Brendan put an arm over her shoulder and she breathed in his musk.

"Come on," he said, "let me buy you a coffee."

***

"Urgh," Brendan said, "how *tacky*."

When Vicky looked up at the coffee shop's sign, she couldn't disagree with him. The flashing neon letters had been written in joined up writing. It read 'Caffeine'. Smoke curled from the back of the 'C' like the smoke from a car's tyres; almost as if the drink would turbo charge you for the rest of your day.

Despite the tacky veneer, the sight of the shop made Vicky's mouth water as she anticipated a strong and hot cup. "They make a *great* coffee though. And it's the most efficient coffee shop in the city."

Vicky led the way and put her bankcard into the machine as soon as she'd entered the shop. She ordered her coffee, and then ordered Brendan's. Black no sugar; the man never changed his mind.

When Vicky stepped onto the conveyor belt, she gripped the moving handrail that ran along beside it. Made from rubber, she held it for balance and turned to Brendan, who'd stepped on behind her.

The pair made small talk as the belt weaved a mazy path through the shop. They had people both in front and behind them. Their chattering voices joined the hiss of steam from the coffee machines. The baristas moved like they'd mainlined the product. Each one ran from one machine to the next as they prepared one of the many coffees on offer.

Most businesses in the food and drink industry tried to keep things simple for efficiency, but coffee shops seemed to go the other way. A new coffee came out every week. *Gingerbread dry*

Grande latte Milano froth monster seemed to be the latest. Vicky often felt like she needed to learn another language to order exactly what she wanted. Instead, she always opted for a gingerbread latte.

"The conveyor belt never stops," Vicky said as she watched two baristas collide when their paths crossed behind the counter. "It's their policy. If they have to stop the belt, everyone on it gets the cost of their coffee refunded. If they don't stop the belt and your coffee is either made wrong, or simply isn't ready, the entire shop gets free coffee."

With a limp jaw, Brendan watched the other people on the belt. Some of them shouted at the baristas like they were angry with them. Some tried to distract them with charm.

After she'd given him a few seconds to digest the chaos, Vicky said, "I even saw someone flash their tits at them once."

"All to distract them?"

"Yep."

"So they could get free coffee?"

"Yep."

Brendan shook his head. "And has it ever worked?"

"*No!* Like fuck. I think that's why people are so desperate to make it happen. Bragging rights or something like that. *Where were you when Summit City opened? Where were you when the cold war started? Where were you when Caffeine's conveyor belt stopped?*"

Brendan shook his head as he watched the chaos. "All of this effort for a free coffee."

***

The coffee cup's exterior remained cool in Vicky's hand when they stepped out of *Caffeine*. The design had been the brainchild of a Swedish scientist and had made him a millionaire overnight. It managed to keep the outside of the cup cool while the coffee inside stayed hot. It had revolutionised coffee drinking.

After he'd glanced around them, Brendan grabbed Vicky's hand and pulled her over to one of the stone benches in the square. It faced both the Alpha Tower and the only water fountain in the area.

Vicky looked across at her lover. "What's up? You seem distracted."

A sip of his coffee and Brendan looked around them again with a deep frown. "Since you've told me about the, you know, *virus* in the tower."

Vicky's heart raced and she looked around too. If someone heard that ... "Please don't mention it so explicitly again."

After he dipped a subtle nod, Brendan continued. "I've been trying to find a way to make your problem go away for you and I think I've found one."

"That's *impossible*, there's *nothing* we can do about it."

"Actually, I think there is. I know some people who could jeopardise it and put the experiments back by years, if not forever."

Vicky had never seen Brendan like this. The man always had a serious side, but he had something almost cold about him that day.

"What kind of people do you know? And what if it goes wrong?"

"These people don't get shit wrong. Trust me. Do you want me to help?"

With the sweet yet bitter taste of gingerbread latte in her mouth, Vicky's throat dried and the first rush of caffeine pulled her stomach tight. She looked into Brendan's icy stare and shook where she sat. After another hit of the hot liquid, she drew a deep breath. When she looked back at Brendan, his eyes had softened a little.

"It's cool either way," he said.

Many innocent people could die when the virus got out. And that was the thing. The virus *would* get out. Vicky nodded. "Yes please, Brendan; I want you to help."

Chapter Eleven

The *crack* of the mobile phone as it hit the ground echoed through Rhys' head long after the sound of it had died. He stared down at the broken device on the driveway. *What an idiot*! He held his breath when he looked up and scanned the dark neighbourhood. The shadows could have contained anything, but what he could see seemed clear. Were it not for Larissa's quick breaths as she recovered from her fight then the street would have been silent.

He felt Larissa's glare burn into the side of his face, and when he finally looked at her, he shrugged. "Okay, so that wasn't one of my brightest ideas."

Larissa looked around as if to make a point. "You *reckon*? Why don't you start your own one-man band to see if you can get any more of the diseased to come out of their houses?"

Even when she had a valid point, she delivered it in a way that made Rhys want to punch her in the face. With his fists balled, he took a calming breath. It did little to satiate his desire for violence.

After a few seconds, he bent down and pulled the trousers off one of the fallen diseased.

"What the fuck are you doing now?" Larissa said.

Rhys didn't reply. Instead, he wrapped the trousers around one of his metal stool legs, both of which protruded like flagpoles from the two diseased he'd killed. Both had been driven through each creature's head so the entire shaft had turned slick with blood and black slime. Rhys wiped the first one clean. "There's no way I'm holding these poles with all this gunk on them."

Larissa didn't respond. Instead, she pulled the shirt off one of the diseased she'd killed and did the same with her broken stool legs.

Rhys couldn't help but look down at the woman Larissa had taken the shirt from. A toned body, he could almost forget about the pulped face and reek of rot. His stomach turned. Who was he kidding?

"Vicky told me the disease is only passed through saliva, but I'm not taking any risks."

Larissa seemed to tense up at the mention of Vicky. She didn't reply as she went more vigorously at her task.

***

After the pair had cleaned their weapons, Rhys looked around again. The neighbourhood stood as quiet now as it had before. The temperature had dropped by a few degrees. A slight gust rode the night air, which bit through Rhys' shirt and made him clench both his jaw and tighten the muscles of his torso. "We need to find a phone," he said. "One that we can *actually* use."

With no streetlights, the shadows seemed to spread out like an oil spill with every passing minute and ate into what little light the slim moon provided. Every window in every house sat as a black hole. If anything stirred inside, Rhys and Larissa had no chance of seeing it.

Rhys looked at the window the diseased had leapt through to get at him. Glass remained in the frame as jagged shards. "I'm guessing there's no more diseased in this house. Surely, they would have jumped out of the window by now if there were. I think we should start our search here."

Each house on the street seemed to have been built from the same plan. Each had a sloped driveway with a garage at the top. The front door sat next to the garage on every house. The only thing that marked out the one in front of them was the phone number painted in blood on the white garage door. Well, that and the huge splash of crimson next to it.

Rhys walked up to the front door and pushed the handle down. The door didn't move. Of course it didn't because that would have been too damn easy. Another look around the quiet neighbourhood and Rhys said, "I don't like it here."

Larissa didn't reply, and when a strong gust of wind flew through the street, she hugged herself tightly.

"Let's go around the back," Rhys said. "Hopefully they've left *that* door unlocked."

An alleyway led to the back garden and a tall gate barred the way. When Rhys pressed the latch, the gate didn't budge. He reached over the top and slid a bolt free, allowing the gate to open. He stepped through with Larissa close behind him.

Unlike the front, the back garden showed serious signs of neglect. An old fridge lay on its side in the corner by a dilapidated shed. A huge rabbit hutch took up the rest of the space. From a quick count, Rhys saw at least seven furry shapes as they shifted around in the tight wooden hutch. They'd starve pretty quickly without human aid. If he let them out when he left, at least they'd have a fighting chance at survival. Despite the mess of the back garden, the concrete path that led to the back door remained unobscured, so Rhys headed down it.

As he walked, Rhys held his breath. The near silence called every one of his steps out no matter how lightly he trod. When he got to the back door, he bit down on his bottom lip and pushed the handle down. It creaked and Rhys' pulse raced. When he'd pushed it all the way down, he put a small amount of pressure on the door and it swung open into the house.

The stench of the diseased rushed out like heat from an oven and hit Rhys in the face. He stepped back and held his nose. "Fuck." He looked around to see Larissa, tight-lipped and focused entirely on him. "You need to be ready for this; it fucking *stinks* in there."

Her dark bob swayed as she nodded.

One last gasp of fresh air and Rhys stepped through the doorway.

Like the outside, the house stood silent. Rhys' feet tapped against the wood laminate floor when he walked down the corridor. His heart beat out of control as the darkness smothered him. A second later, he heard a noise like a pig at a trough. He froze and raised a hand to halt Larissa.

Larissa stopped.

Rhys leaned so close to his ex-wife he could smell the slight tang of sweat on her skin. The familiar scent took him back to well before Flynn arrived when they had Sunday morning lie-ins and sex after a night out. "The kitchen," Rhys whispered. "Whatever it is, it's coming from the kitchen."

After he'd raised both of his spear-like stool legs, he walked toward the sound.

Larissa followed, the gentle pad of her feet in time with his own.

As they got close, the snarls and growls of a diseased became clearer. It sounded like there was just one of them.

By the time he'd gotten to the kitchen door, sweat coated Rhys' palms and the spears shook in his moist grip. The snarls and growls of the diseased had grown louder, as if the creature sensed their arrival, but it hadn't moved yet.

When Rhys poked his head around the corner both the smell and sight hit him at once and he heaved.

The diseased lay on the ground with a wheelchair toppled on its side. With half of its face torn open it stared fury at Rhys. It snapped and groaned and reached out to him, but it couldn't move the lower half of its body.

When it opened its mouth and took a deep, breath Rhys ran forward and drove both stool legs into its face. The wet *shunk* of both poles cut the creature's scream off before it could release it. A look of horror had frozen on its face. Its mouth hung wide open and its black tongue lolled out.

Two moist *schlops* as Rhys pulled each spear free and he looked at the fallen wheelchair. It had a large handbag hooked over one of the handles so he stepped over the corpse and picked it up.

Heavier than he'd expected, Rhys lifted the bag up onto the kitchen table and tipped the contents across it. A phone spilled out amongst the assortment of make-up, a purse, a compact mirror, a novel, and a whole host of other useless items. Rhys grabbed it, pressed the button, and the screen lit up. "It's an *older* model, Larissa." In his excitement, he'd spoken a bit too loudly.

Larissa remained by the kitchen doorway and stared at the dead woman.

Rhys dropped down next to the corpse, pushed her finger to the phone's screen, and watched the thing unlock.

A notepad and pen had fallen out of the woman's handbag, so Rhys took the leaves from his pocket, wrote down Vicky's phone number, and dialled it.

Larissa still hadn't moved. She watched on with her mouth open wide and her tense shoulders lifted into her neck.

A warm beep pulsed in Rhys' ear and he pulled the phone away from his face to look at the bright screen. "Fuck it. It's not connecting, even though it has full service." After he'd redialled and got the same result, Rhys sighed. "It won't connect us. She must be in a bad area. At least the networks are still working, I suppose. I'm guessing that means the world hasn't fallen apart just yet. If we can find them and get through London before the disease catches up with us, we'll be home free."

Larissa looked around the kitchen before she finally spoke. "So what do we do? Wait here until she calls back?"

Before Rhys could answer her, the back garden gate crashed open. His heart boomed and he crouched down below the window. When he saw Larissa had also dropped to the floor he crawled across the kitchen, poked his head out, and peered down the hallway at the back door.

Six diseased had entered the back garden. They moved much slower than he'd ever seen them walk. In single file, they headed straight for the rabbit hutch.

The one at the front, a girl who couldn't have been any older than about sixteen, tried several times before she finally beat her clumsiness and lifted the top of the hutch open.

She let out a slight growl as she leaned forward. When she stood up again the dark form of a rabbit twisted in her grip. The groans and grumblings of agitation rippled through the pack as she passed the rabbit to the diseased next to her.

The small animal kicked and fought as it moved all the way down the line to the creature at the back.

While the one at the front selected another rabbit Rhys watched the one at the back lift the first one to its mouth. The black furry animal continued to fight until the diseased bit into its neck. A light *pop* of what must have been the rabbit's windpipe and the thing fell limp.

After the diseased had taken a bite from it, the rabbit's insides drawing a line from its belly to the diseased's mouth, it passed the dead creature onto another one of the group.

The next diseased bit a chunk from it as well.

Rhys jumped when Larissa spoke. He didn't realise how close she'd gotten to him. "What the fuck are they doing, Rhys?"

Unable to take his eyes from the scene outside, Rhys finally found the words. "They're *feeding*. It's what I thought when I saw the policewoman. It looks like they've learned how to survive."

Chapter Twelve

Five Days Ago

Vicky's pulse raced and she struggled to breathe. An invisible hand gripped her neck and squeezed as she looked up at the security cameras in the hallway before she slipped into the room. Building management gave her free reign of the Alpha Tower, except for the penthouse suite. She needed that freedom because light bulbs needed to be checked and faults needed to be addressed. If anyone stopped her, she had a legitimate reason to be there; it was tenuous, but legitimate all the same.

She may have been away from the cameras in the staff room, but if someone came in to find her checking the staff rota, she'd be fucked. Light bulbs and electrical points were fine, but confidential paperwork was a whole other issue. And it wasn't just any staff rota—she needed to see the rota for the security guards. Sweat stood on her brow as she closed the door behind her and walked over to the shift manager's desk.

With shaking hands and the reek of coffee heavy in the air, Vicky opened the shift manager's drawer and pulled out the red rota file. Although it worked in her favour today, it seemed ridiculous that they still had to have the rota on paper. Every other building in the city used an electronic system, but because of hackers, the Alpha Tower couldn't risk it.

The click of footsteps sounded outside and Vicky froze. She kept a hold of the file. No point in trying to hide because she had nowhere to go, and the rush to put it back would make a noise that would alert the people. If they entered the room, she'd have to 'fess up and their plan would be fucked at the first hurdle. After a dry gulp, Vicky continued to watch the back of the currently closed door. *Please let them go past. Please.*

Two pairs of heels clicked in time as they got closer to the room. Each click snapped through Vicky and wound her body tighter than the one before. As they neared the door, an urge overwhelmed Vicky to give herself over at that moment. If she walked outside now then maybe they'd go easier on her. She saw herself being caught red-handed; anything had to be better than that.

Although, what would she tell them? That the man she loved planned an act against them, against the state. Besides, she was already an accomplice and no amount of confessing would change that. A chill sank through her as if her blood had frozen. Whether she thought of herself as one or not, she would be judged as a terrorist. With a policy of zero tolerance when it came to terrorism, she wouldn't stand a fucking chance. Better to go down in flames now than with a whimper as she cowered in the shadow of some over-fed judge.

The heels *clicked* against the hard floor and Vicky remained frozen to the spot. Sweat ran down her back as she waited for the handle to drop.

But the clicks went straight past.

As she listened to the people continue down the corridor, Vicky released a heavy sigh. Her hands slick with sweat, she looked down at the file. She could forget all this nonsense and tell Brendan it didn't matter, but the consequences of that could be catastrophic too, and not just for her. If she didn't stop the virus' creation, she'd have to live with the fact that she could have stopped the death of millions. The time for debate had passed. She'd started down this road so she needed to keep going. A shake of her head and Vicky flipped the file open. She took a photo of the shift rota with her phone and sent it to Brendan.

Once the message had sent, she carefully placed the file back in the drawer and walked over to the door.

After she'd drawn a deep breath, she opened it and strode back into the hallway as if she had nothing to hide.

***

Between the hours of twelve and two, you couldn't move for people in the canteen. It presented the perfect opportunity.

Nausea turned knots in Vicky's stomach as she queued with a plate of food. The greasy smell of her sausages and chips overwhelmed her and forced her tongue against the roof of her mouth. The collective chat from the diners turned into white noise in the high-ceilinged room. The heat in the canteen didn't help either. The middle of summer, but with heavy rainfall, they'd kept the windows closed. Humidity seemed to coat everything and made it impossible to see outside. The air had thickened to the point where it became hard to breathe and the place felt like a damn rainforest.

Vicky had seen the woman next to her around, but she didn't know her well. Good job really, considering what she had planned for her.

As they slid their trays toward the tills at the end of the line, Vicky looked down at the woman's white security card. Low level, but enough for what she needed. Also, it meant the owner would be much less likely to guard it. And who cared if a basic card went missing? It happened all the time. Security could issue her a new one after the obligatory bollocking. One of the main failings with the Alpha Tower's security was that it took a week to cancel a missing card. A glitch in the system that no one had thought to fix and not many people knew about. Artem did, which in turn meant Vicky did. The week's grace they'd have on the card gave them plenty of time.

With the woman engaged in a conversation with her friend, Vicky waited until they seemed particularly engrossed in their gossip before she pretended to straighten her own tray. As she reached across, she stole the security card.

After a couple more seconds she tutted aloud to herself, shook her head, and said, "Damn it. I need to get a drink."

She rolled her eyes at the man behind her and said, "You go in front of me; I need to pick up a few more bits."

Without a word, the man moved past her and Vicky walked back to the self-serving section of the canteen.

With everyone more involved in their food than their surroundings, Vicky managed to put her tray down unnoticed and leave it as she walked out of the sweaty building.

***

The second Vicky stepped out of the canteen, she saw Artem. She couldn't pass up the opportunity so she raised her hand in the air and called out, "Artem." She then ran to catch up with him and fell into stride beside him.

"Where are you going?"

"Back to the security room," Artem said. His green eyes looked from side to side. "Why?"

"Oh, no reason."

"You just like walking along the corridors next to people, huh?"

Vicky laughed with a little too much enthusiasm and Artem looked at her like she'd lost her mind. "Sorry," she said as she pulled her hair away from her face. "I suppose I just wanted to see how you are."

"I'm fine."

"And work?"

"That's fine."

"You must get bored down in the security room on your own."

"There's two of us down there."

"Always two?"

"Yes. What's with all the questions, Vicky?"

Vicky pretended to blush. "Sorry, Artem, I just feel a bit awkward around you sometimes is all. I feel like we should talk because I don't want it to be weird … but you've seen me naked so I suppose it *is* kind of weird."

Artem's jaw fell limp and he didn't respond. Vicky patted

him on the shoulder, turned around, and walked away. If in doubt, mention sex. She smirked to herself as she left him behind.

***

As Vicky walked back to her office, the stolen security card in her top pocket seemed to treble in weight. With one of the cleaner's cupboards up on her right, she nipped into it and closed the door. This was another room she could justify being in. After all, the cleaners needed to have enough supplies.

The closet was so dark she couldn't see an inch in front of her face and the stench of bleach seemed to weave into the fabric of her being. The reek of it would be stuck to her for days. Vicky removed the card from her pocket and slipped it into her knickers. Surely, they wouldn't even search anyone for such a low-level card, but if they did …

Just before Vicky left the cupboard, she heard the voices of two men. No more than the size of a toilet cubicle, the small space had paper-thin walls. Vicky tried to think where she was in relation to the rest of the building. When it hit her, she gasped. The men she could hear were in the high-security conference room on that floor. Did the building's architects realise they'd designed the perfect listening post?

Vicky reached out in the dark for the back of the cupboard. When she caught a broom handle, she moved it aside and stepped forward. Each blind step made her stomach lurch. At some point, she'd stand on something and give the game away. However, when she reached out again her fingertips caught the back of the cupboard. Vicky moved closer, pressed her face against the cool wall, and listened.

"So we think if we infect a person it would make them highly dangerous. Just *one* would be enough to bring down an *entire* country. The perfect weapon! And here's the good part, the virus will stop them swimming or climbing. They'll lose enough coordination to prevent that. Sure, they'll be super fast, but—"

"They won't be able get back to The West."

"Exactly."

"Excellent. And when do you think it will be ready?"

"Well, there's one thing we need to do."

"Oh?"

"We need to test it. We need to infect someone. I was thinking of doing it next Monday. The good thing about that is it will allow me to test the vaccine too. I'm hoping to turn her, assess her, and then turn her back."

"Her?"

"Alice."

"*Your wife?*"

Vicky could almost hear the man grin when he said, "That's how confident I am I can make this work."

Silence hung between the two men, and Vicky's pulse throbbed so hard that her face swelled with it.

Finally, the man who clearly made the decisions sighed and said, "Okay. I'm going to put faith in you on this one, John. Don't let me down."

"Don't worry," John said, "I won't."

Any doubt Vicky had about their plans vanished in that moment. This had to end. *Now.*

Chapter Thirteen

Rhys watched the diseased girl pull the final rabbit from the hutch and revulsion writhed through him. A slow shiver ran the length of his body as he watched the white furry creature kick and twist more than any of the others had before it. "It obviously knows what's going to happen to it," Rhys said.

The diseased girl didn't pass this one back. Instead, she bit into the thing's neck herself. Because the door to the back garden stood slightly ajar, it made the crunch of the rabbit's windpipe crystal clear. The smell of the diseased outside had found its way in too; or maybe Rhys had become more aware of the reek that already existed in the house.

Each diseased had its own unique wound, and even in the darkness of night the little light cast from the moon glistened off the septic gashes and cuts. Rhys screwed his face up at the sight of them.

"But why are they killing the rabbits and not eating them?" Larissa asked.

Rhys watched the diseased girl drop her recently killed rabbit to the ground onto the pile of others already there. The first one had been passed around, and they'd all taken a bite, but every other one had been executed and discarded.

Before Rhys could respond, the diseased each picked up a rabbit or two from the pile. Rhys' breath caught in his throat and he spoke in no more than a whisper. "Oh my God."

"What?"

"They're *saving* food for later. It's so strange to see them like this. If they know a human's nearby, they lose their shit and can't focus on anything but attacking them. But when they're not they find sustenance and work together as a team. The police officer back out on the road was the first person I'd seen actually eaten by the diseased. Before then they seemed to bite people, infect them, and then leave them to change."

Rhys' skin crawled as he watched the diseased leave the garden. Some of them took one rabbit, some of them two. The final one, the girl who'd taken them from their hutch in the first place, took the last two and followed the rest of the diseased back out of the gate.

After they'd left, Rhys turned to Larissa. "The virus has the most perfect survival instincts. It only switches on when there are people to—"

"Kill?" Larissa asked.

"Infect. Then as soon as the people have turned, the desire to attack them vanishes. They ate the police because the officers were already dead when they found them. They were a free meal."

A look of horror had drawn Larissa's features long.

"So that means …"

Just the thought of saying it tightened Rhys' stomach. "The disease isn't burning itself out. The virus is built to *survive*."

***

The pair stood in the dark of the house's kitchen and listened to the mob walk away. Fortunately, they went back the way they came in. Fuck knows what Rhys and Larissa would have done had they decided to enter the house.

After a few minutes, Rhys pulled the phone from his pocket and unlocked it with the dead woman's fingerprint. He tried Vicky again.

The same warm pulse told him the call couldn't be connected. "Fuck it." He pulled the phone away from his ear and looked at the bright screen like he'd done the first time around. The thing still had full service.

"You can't get through?" Larissa asked.

After a deep sigh, Rhys shook his head. "No. But we can't hang around here and wait for Vicky to be in an area where she has service. If the diseased are being drawn to Summit City, we need to keep moving. I don't think London's fallen yet, and I *certainly* don't want to be there when it does."

At that moment, Rhys saw the key rack that had been screwed into the kitchen wall. Shaped like a massive brass key itself, several sets dangled down from the small hooks. He walked over and took the only car key there. Fuck knows what all the others did.

When he turned back to Larissa, he saw her staring at the dead woman on the floor. When she looked up, confusion skewed her features. She pointed down at the woman, "But what about …?"

A wooden knife block sat on the kitchen worktop and Rhys

slid the biggest knife he could from it. A heavy chopping knife, he felt the weight of it sit in his hand like an extension of his arm. The high-quality blade probably cost a small fortune.

"What are you …?"

But before Larissa could finish her sentence, Rhys had dropped down into a hunch. If he didn't do it now, he'd never do it. One wide swing of the knife and he chopped off the four fingers on the woman's right hand with a *shunk*. He left her with four bloody stumps and a thumb.

From the way Larissa jumped and clapped her hand over her mouth, Rhys had expected her to scream, but she didn't. With the bottom half of her face covered, her wide green eyes stood out in the dark as she stared down.

Cold and soft, Rhys lifted the woman's index finger and tested it against the phone. It unlocked it still. He then slipped the digit into his top pocket. Nausea ran through him and he wore a layer of sweat like a second skin, but he couldn't see any other way to make the phone work and they didn't have time to fuck about.

After he'd stood up, Rhys felt the weight of the knife in his hand again. Tempting, but … he put it down on the kitchen table. He'd have to get too close to the fuckers for it to be of any use. The stool legs would have to do for the time being.

"Come on then," he said as he passed the car keys to Larissa.

"You want *me* to drive?"

"I need to call Vicky."

For a second Larissa looked as if she wanted to argue with him. She then dipped a tight nod. "Okay, let's get the fuck out of here. Let's get to London before the diseased do."

***

The garage door creaked and groaned when Rhys opened it to reveal the car inside. Once he had it fully lifted, he paused and listened for a moment. He couldn't hear the footfalls of the diseased and nothing moved in the deep shadows. The ones with the rabbits must have moved on already and the rest of the residents had to be on their way to Summit City. A glance in the direction of the burning towers and he watched the orange glow for a second. The hypnotic effect that flames had over humans clearly hadn't been lost when the virus infected a person. Although what they hoped to find when they got there …

Larissa pulled the car out onto the driveway and Rhys jumped in. Once in the passenger seat, he used the woman's finger to unlock the phone again. He then tried Vicky.

Nothing.

The two beams from the car's headlights lit up the street. "It seems quiet," Larissa said as she scanned the road in front of her. "I *don't* like it."

"Don't worry, everything will be fine. It's quiet because the diseased have all headed the other way."

After Larissa had thrown a dark stare at Rhys, she looked ahead again. "So what you're saying is we can be guided by *your* intuition and faith, but when I have a gut feeling we need to ignore it? All that matters is you feel good about something, yeah? *Just* so I can get it straight."

Rhys ignored her facetious questions. Truth be told, he felt far from good about driving into London, but they had to remain positive and they had no other options.

Larissa spoke through clenched teeth and her frown deepened. "I *hate* that our boy's with a woman I don't know or trust."

What felt like a natural reaction to defend Vicky rose up in Rhys, but he swallowed it down. "Me too. I hate it too."

Rhys saw Larissa in his peripheral vision. She looked at him, back to the road, at him again, and back to the road again.

He knew her well enough to hear the question before she'd asked it. 'Why the fuck did you leave him with her then?' But she kept it to herself. The arguments got them nowhere so Rhys kept his mouth shut too and simply watched the road ahead.

They started up a long, straight hill when he finally spoke. "I'm sorry," he said. "I fucked up. I thought I was doing the right thing."

Before Larissa could respond, a silhouette appeared at the top of the hill. Clumsy and with its arms flailing it ran straight for the car.

To have the thing bare down on them with such malicious intent took Rhys' breath for a second. Even though he'd seen it countless times already, he certainly hadn't desensitised to the horror that bore down on them. "It's fine," he said as he watched the monster, a warble in his voice. "One of them is no match for a car."

"What about two?" Larissa said. She'd already eased off the gas as another silhouette appeared.

Before Rhys could reply, another one appeared.

And then another.

Larissa stopped the car.

Suddenly a crowd as wide as the road raced over the brow of the hill. The chaotic collection of rage had just one focus, the bright headlights that lit up the street. Rhys' heart beat in his neck as he watched the furious mob. His mouth dried and his breaths grew shallow. "Fuck!"

Chapter Fourteen

About twelve hours ago

A clipboard and a checklist always made someone look busy and like they belonged. Most buildings used tablets, but not the Alpha Tower; you couldn't hack a paper checklist. They'd checked all the fixtures and fittings a couple of days ago and another check didn't need to be done for a week or so. But most people would have no idea, which gave Vicky the chance to move around the Alpha Tower's foyer without raising suspicion.

As she pretended to check every light bulb in the place, she kept her attention on the front doors. The huge clock on the wall read eleven fifty-eight. At twelve o'clock, the shifts switched around. The low-level buzz of anxiety that had resided inside of her for several days rose up a notch, and no matter how many times she swallowed, her nausea would not be abated.

When the toilet doors opened, Vicky's pulse spiked. Two men emerged in the uniforms she'd stolen. They strode toward the front door and looked like any two security guards about to change shift would.

Vicky didn't recognise the two tall men and they wouldn't know her either. Thank God, Brendan hadn't chosen to be one of them. One had pulled out at the last minute and it looked like he may have to step in, but they fortunately found a replacement. Already wound up so tight she could snap, she didn't need to see Brendan putting his life in danger as well.

When one of the men opened the door to let the other one out, Vicky caught sight of the security guards outside. Both of them turned to look at the men.

The fake security guards stepped outside and Vicky watched them talk to one another for a second before the front door shut on them. Despite the porthole window in the door, she couldn't see through it to the men on the other side.

The doors then opened again and the two security guards who had been on shift entered the foyer. They must have fallen for it. They obviously didn't see their replacements using a stolen security card.

Vicky glanced at the clock again. Too soon and the current guards would have been suspicious. Too late and the real guards for the next shift would have appeared. They had about a minute to make this work.

At that moment, Brendan walked into the foyer and Vicky lost her breath.

With his shoulders back and his chin raised, he walked with his usual confidence. He looked like he belonged and paid Vicky no attention.

To distract herself, Vicky hunched down to check the power outlets near to where she stood, although most of her focus remained on the man she loved as he walked across the vast open space to the lifts. He had a card that gave him clearance to the control room. That's all he'd asked for. Sure, it didn't feel great that Vicky had stolen Artem's card, especially when she saw the panic on his face when he realised it had gone, but he should have looked after it. She had more concern about when he would report it missing. Nobody would give a shit about the low-level card she stole in the canteen, but one that accessed the building's security would raise alarm. It would also see Artem fired, which must have been why he hadn't reported it yet. Maybe he hoped it would turn up.

The second the lift doors closed on Brendan, the ones next to him let out a light *ping*. Two security guards stepped out. Bang on time, the twelve o'clock shift had arrived.

The two uniformed men strode across the foyer to the front doors. Vicky pretended to write, but her hand shook so badly she wasn't able to make a legible mark. When she looked back up at the men, one of them glanced her way. She quickly averted her gaze.

Another quick glance and she saw the man had also looked away.

Crouched closer to the doors than she had been on the first switch over, Vicky listened to the men's conversation.

"It's time to switch shifts."

"What do you mean? We've *only* just got here."

"But it's *our* shift now."

"No it's not. We were told to do today, weren't we, Bill?"

Bill nodded. "Yeah, I dunno what the mix up is, boys. Why don't you go and find out while we hold the fort?"

When the men turned back into the foyer, Vicky dropped

her eyes to her clipboard again. A shake ran through her entire body and she had to lean against a wall so she didn't fall from her crouch. She kept her attention down as the men passed her on their way back to the lift.

When she heard the *ping* of the lift door, she looked up again to watch the lift close on the two legitimate guards. A glance at the main entrance and she saw the face of one of the fake guards at the porthole window as he watched the lift the two men had entered.

His face then vanished and Vicky knew the men would walk away at that point. They'd stood guard while Brendan entered just to avoid any unnecessary suspicion. They'd now done their job. Brendan hadn't told Vicky what would happen next. The less she knew the better.

When Vicky looked down, she saw she'd scribbled nonsense all over the checklist. Not that it mattered anymore. The time to regret her actions had passed. This thing would happen now whether she liked it or not.

Chapter Fifteen

"Come *on*!" Rhys shouted as he watched the mob dash down the hill. Their blood lust oozed from them as a shared intention. Ruthless in their desire to get at Rhys and Larissa, they shoved and pushed one another aside as they ran.

Larissa snapped the car into reverse, spun the wheels as she accelerated backwards, and turned the steering wheel to a full left lock.

The car jolted when they smashed into the curb on the other side of the road and a deep *thunk* vibrated through Rhys' seat.

"Steady on," Rhys said. "We want this car in one piece so it can get us out of here." More than just a crowd of silhouettes, Rhys now heard their collective fury as it made its way down the hill.

Larissa lurched the car forward and hit the curb on the other side of the road. The impact threw Rhys toward the windscreen.

A glance up the road and Rhys saw the diseased had halved the distance between them since she'd put it into reverse. Panic clattered through him. "Come on, come on, *come on*."

Red faced and wide-eyed, Larissa turned on Rhys. "You're

not fucking *helping.*" Veins stood out on her forehead and she looked ready to swing for him. She shoved it into reverse again and whacked the curb for a third time.

Rhys looked between Larissa, who shook so badly she struggled to put it back into first, and the diseased behind who were now less than ten metres away from them.

Another lurch forward and Larissa stalled.

Rhys bit his bottom lip as he watched her fumble for the start button and bounced up and down on his seat.

Five metres.

Larissa revved the engine so hard it drowned out the hellish sound of the diseased before she wheel-spun away. The front of the car seemed to bounce on the spot as a shudder ripped through the vehicle.

The lead diseased slapped the back of the car and got so close Rhys saw its bloody eyes through the back window. Several more caught up and smacked the car's bodywork.

For the next few seconds, Rhys watched the diseased ease up as the gap between them grew. The red glow from the car's taillights showed the slumped forms of defeat. They knew when they were beat. When he turned back around, he sniffed the acrid smell of the burned clutch and looked at Larissa. She panted as she hunched over the wheel. "Good work," he said as a relieved sigh.

"You *didn't* fucking help. *Why* did you shout at me?"

"I'm sorry. I panicked."

"Yeah, you did." A dark frown crushed her face as she continued to stare straight ahead.

Rhys reached across and rubbed her left shoulder. The knot

of tension eased a little at his touch.

It took Rhys several more deep breaths to exorcise his adrenaline-induced shakes. He pulled the phone and the dead lady's severed finger from his pocket. The cold digit brought a rich shot of acidic rot with it. He screwed his nose up and looked to see Larissa had the same reaction to the smell.

"Fucking thing stinks."

Larissa didn't reply. Instead, she focused on the road ahead as she tore through the small town's tight streets.

As she negotiated their escape route with sharp turns, Rhys snapped one way and then the other. He had to hold the phone with both hands to steady it enough for him to hit redial. He lifted the phone to his ear and the purr of a ring tone made him straighten in his seat.

"It's *ringing*."

Larissa eased off slightly and looked across at him.

At that precise moment, a diseased sprung from the darkness to be lit up by the car's headlights. Rhys pulled his legs up in the chair and Larissa screamed as they crashed straight into it. The *thud* struck through the car like a sledgehammer blow and the diseased man spun away into the darkness on Larissa's side of the car.

With the phone to his ear still, Rhys nodded ahead. "Keep your eyes on the road!"

Although Larissa replied, Rhys didn't hear it because Vicky answered the phone at that moment.

"Hello."

"Vicky? Where the fuck are you?"

She breathed heavily down the phone and lowered her voice.

"I'm trying to get away from Brendan. I can't see him, but I know he hasn't given up on our trail. The guy's a psychopath."

The scream of the diseased near Vicky roared so loudly it sent needles of pain into Rhys' eardrum. He had to pull the phone away from his face. When he put it back, he listened to the chaos that clearly surrounded her.

"Is it bad where you are too?" he asked.

For a moment, Vicky didn't reply. After several heavy breaths she finally said, "London's fallen, Rhys. It's fucked. When I was waiting for you in the police car, I saw a helicopter fly over with a cage of those creatures. I think they've dropped the diseased into London. Flynn and I are going to have to turn around and head back toward Summit City."

"Flynn's okay, is he?"

Larissa slowed down some more.

"He's fine."

A look across at his ex-wife and Rhys nodded at her.

"Let me speak to him," Larissa said as she reached for the phone. The car swerved and she almost lost control.

Rhys pulled away. "Focus on driving, Larissa. Vicky, we need to think of somewhere we can meet."

"I agree. We need to go south to get away from London. How about Biggin Hill Airport? There's an old industrial estate next to it. I can't imagine there'll be many of the diseased there."

More screams hurt Rhys' ear.

"Okay," Rhys said, "we can get to Biggin Hill Airport. Can you meet us there in an hour?"

Vicky fought for breath and then finally said, "Yes, I can."

"Can we speak to Flynn?"

Although Vicky didn't reply, Rhys heard her pass the phone to his son.

"Dad?"

"Flynn, are you okay, mate?"

"I'm *scared*, Dad."

"It'll be okay. Just do what Vicky says and you'll be okay."

"Like fuck will he be okay," Larissa said and ripped the phone from Rhys' hand. "Flynn, baby."

Despite the short distance between them, Rhys heard the beeps before she'd said anything.

Larissa looked at the phone. "The connection dropped."

Chapter Sixteen

About twelve hours ago

They hadn't discussed what would happen next and they hadn't discussed what Vicky should do at this point either. She'd make sure the fake guards had a minute before the real guards turned up so they could let Brendan in. She'd distract the real guards if necessary, and then she'd … what the fuck *would* she do?

Still in the foyer of the Alpha Tower, Vicky looked around. Surely someone had rumbled her. What if Brendan didn't destroy the CCTV footage like he'd promised? Someone would see her in the foyer, aimless with a stupid clipboard. They'd be bound to review the footage from the day.

Vicky hunched down again with her clipboard and wrote more nonsense on the form. She'd have to replace it with a legit one later. If they asked to see her paper trail, they'd uncover the ramblings of a mad woman … or a terrorist.

Adrenaline surged through Vicky's blood as she remained hunched by the socket. It didn't take anybody that long to examine a plug socket. Not even Vicky.

When she stood up she nearly fell down again.

Fear had turned her legs bandy as she walked across the foyer. If she looked at the cameras now, it would be obvious she had something to hide. She had to style it out, walk like she owned the place, and get back to her office as soon as fucking possible.

As she crossed the space, the lift doors pinged and the two legitimate security guards from a few minutes before returned. They marched across the room and their heels clicked in unison with one another's.

When one of them opened the door, his loud voice echoed in the open space. "Where are they?"

A lady in her mid to late forties entered the building and the security guard stepped in front of her. "Have *you* seen them?"

"Who?"

"The two security guards."

The woman looked at the security guard and then at his colleague next to him. Although her mouth moved up and down, she didn't say anything.

"*Fine*," the guard said, "show me your pass."

The woman did as she'd been ordered and then moved on when the guard let her through.

The first guard must have been the senior of the two because he lifted his walkie-talkie and said, "Check the labs. Check the labs *now*."

The other guard made eye contact with Vicky. It was the same one who had looked at her before. Her pulse soared and every part of her screamed that she should run, but she wouldn't make it to the end of the foyer before the guy caught up with her. She'd worn her trainers to work that day, but the guys in security were serious athletes.

"You," the guard said. Vicky pointed at herself and he nodded. "Yep. You were down here when the two fake guards were on watch. What did you see?"

Her body temperature went up by what felt like a thousand degrees and her shirt stuck to her clammy body. "I … uh … I …"

The *ping* of the lift cut through her pathetic response. The gold-plated doors slid open and inside, amongst blood and guts, stood a family of four and two scientists, or rather they *used* to be.

Not anymore.

Chapter Seventeen

"I hate that that *woman* has our boy," Larissa said as she frowned deeper than before and the car sped up.

After he'd looked down at her foot on the accelerator, Rhys said, "She'll look after him. I'm sure of it."

"Forgive me if I don't trust your judgment, Rhys. After all, you *were* the one who left him with her in the first place."

Maybe she had a point. "I did the best I could do at the time. He wanted you back so what else could I have done? I should have fucking left you to die in the city." Before she could answer him, Rhys said, "Anyway, *I* trust Vicky. She's given me no reason to think I shouldn't. Besides, Oscar was a certified lunatic so I can't take his word for anything."

Rhys looked at Larissa's slim hands as they wrung the faux leather steering wheel. She ground her jaw and accelerated even harder than before.

Although Larissa had switched the car's full beams on, their visibility had been seriously reduced by the lack of streetlights now that they were out of the town. Rhys' eyes stung as he stared into the darkness, afraid to blink. Another glance at her accelerator foot and he said, "You could slow down a little, you know. The last thing we need is another diseased springing us and writing the car off."

"If you're going to criticise my driving, Rhys, why don't *you* do it?"

Despite the tension in the car, Rhys laughed.

Larissa glanced across at him with a hard frown on her face as she barked, "What's so funny?"

"It feels like we never broke up."

"And we wouldn't have if you hadn't fucked another woman."

"Here we go again."

Larissa finally eased off the gas and looked at him. "I'm *sorry*, are you getting bored of talking about how you broke mine *and* Flynn's hearts?"

"Look …"

Larissa glared at him again. "Look *what*?"

"I was scared."

"*Scared*?"

It did sound pathetic. "It was *scary* being a new dad. I freaked out and I fucked up."

Larissa shook her head and the car shook with it. "Oh, well *that's* all right then. Silly me. Everything seems so much clearer now. You lost your bottle a little bit at the prospect of becoming a parent so you decided to go off and fuck some old *tart*."

Her glare took on a new level of malice that made Rhys physically recoil.

"What do you think *I* did when you went off with *her*?"

Any answer would be wrong so Rhys didn't respond.

"I womaned the fuck up and took care of our little boy. You keep giving it the big *I am* about how you've saved me from Building Seventy-two, but we wouldn't have a beautiful little boy that wanted me back if I hadn't been there to change his nappies and read to him at night. You want to know why I fought you for the custody of Flynn?"

When Rhys opened his mouth, Larissa cut him short. "That was a rhetorical question. I fought you because I felt like you didn't deserve to have any part in his life."

Some of the tension appeared to leave Larissa's body as she slumped back in her seat with a sigh. "I've *hated* you for the longest time."

"I understand." Rhys leaned across and squeezed Larissa's shoulder again. "I'm going to be here now. It can't make up for what I've done, but I'll be here whenever you need me. I hope that one day you'll find it in your heart to forgive me."

A tremble took over Larissa's bottom lip and her emerald eyes glazed. When she blinked, a single tear rolled down her cheek. "*Why* did you have to fuck everything up? We could have been great as a family. Even now, with Clive more of a dad than you've ever been, Flynn asks about you. He really needed you."

Grief caught in Rhys' throat as a sharp lump. "He *does*?"

"Of *course* he fucking does." The tears now streamed down Larissa's cheeks. "They say that young kids forget their early years, but Flynn has *never* forgotten you. We leave a photo of you on his bedside table. I wanted to take it down but Clive insisted we left it there."

The air left Rhys' lungs and he couldn't find the words.

"He did it because he felt that Flynn should always make the choice who his parents were. As much as he loved Clive he *always* chose you."

The bubble burst and hot tears ran down Rhys' cheeks. "Why didn't—"

His words were cut dead by a loud *bang!* Rhys looked in front and flinched as a body flew toward him and hit the windscreen. A spider web of cracks popped across the glass and Rhys spun around to see the diseased hit the road behind, jump to its feet, and roar at them before it gave chase.

Larissa weaved her head to try to see as she drove. "I can't see *anything*. The window's fucked, Rhys. I can't see a *damn thing*."

Another loud *bang* and they hit another diseased. It took the same path as the first and hit the windshield with another *crunch*.

More cracks blinded Rhys and Larissa screamed, "Rhys, do something. I *can't* drive like this."

They hit another diseased with yet another loud *thud!*

All the while, Larissa kept her foot down and the car raced through the dark streets. If she had a similar view to Rhys, she couldn't see fuck all at that moment. "Do you think that's the last of 'em?" she asked.

"I dunno, I hope so." Rhys then popped his seatbelt off and lifted his feet up in front of him.

"What are you doing?"

Instead of a reply, Rhys kicked out at the screen. It didn't budge and the shock ran all the way to the base of his back. The pain from his bike accident returned as a numbness at the tops of his legs. With clenched teeth, he growled and kicked out at the window again.

The top left corner came free from the frame.

Rhys kicked again and it came free a little more.

When he kicked again, the entire window moved.

He kicked out one final time and yelled. The window flopped forward. A rush of wind filled the car before the window flipped back into place. "Fuck it."

Another kick and Rhys managed to dislodge the bottom of the window. He then leaned forward, grabbed the screen, and wiggled it to work the bottom corner by Larissa free. It finally came loose and he pulled the window away.

The wind continued to push against the large sheet of glass, but Rhys managed to move it across inch by inch. Once he'd shifted it far enough out of place he pushed it around the side of the car.

The *whoosh* of the window hit the ground and skidded across the road surface before it vanished behind them.

The breezed flapped in Rhys' ears and ruffled his hair. Gone ten in the evening the wind had a sharp bite that it hadn't had earlier that day.

Rhys looked to his right and watched the city burn. He looked ahead again and the coast seemed clear, although they'd lost one of the headlights when they hit the diseased so he couldn't be sure.

Rhys looked to see Larissa's hair tossed about by the strong gusts. She gripped the steering wheel as if it would stop her blowing away. As she stared into the oncoming gale she blinked repeatedly and maintained their fast pace.

Rhys had to shout to be heard. "Well done, 'Rissa." He reached across and stroked her forearm. He'd not called her that in a very long time. "Well done."

Chapter Eighteen

About twelve hours ago

Before the six people in the lift emerged, their screams filled the foyer. Everyone turned to see the nightmare that had just entered their world. As one, each ravenous once human exploded from their confined space and attacked the first person they could. The slap of bodies smashed together and seconds later, they each hit the ground with a series of thuds that ran vibrations through the soles of Vicky's feet. The victims' cries were amplified by the large open space.

The security guard next to Vicky pulled a small black pole from his pocket and snapped his wrist. It turned into a baton as long as his arm. Balled at the end, he raised it above his head and ran forward.

When the second security guard followed the first, Vicky saw her opportunity. She dropped her clipboard and ran out of the tower.

Sure to close the door behind her, Vicky looked out over the quiet square. Many people sat on or around the benches and enjoyed a lunch in the summer sun. After she'd looked back into the Alpha Tower at the chaos that tore through the place, she removed her phone from her pocket and called Brendan.

The wet pulse of the connected phone rang in her ear and Vicky shook as she continued to watch the insanity inside the tower. It had already gotten to the point where she couldn't tell who had the disease and who didn't, although it seemed abundantly clear which side would win. Before long, the entire city would be overrun.

Brendan answered the phone. Out of breath, she could hear his feet hit the ground as he ran.

"Hello?"

"*Brendan*! What shall I do?"

Vicky listened to him run but he didn't reply. "Brendan? Where shall I meet you? Where do you want me to go to?"

A loud explosion shook the ground beneath her feet and Vicky heard it through Brendan's phone too. He was closer to it than her. "Brendan, what's happening? Are you okay?"

Vicky heard Brendan stop running and a car door slammed shut a second later. He gasped for breath down the phone.

"Brendan?"

Vicky heard the screech of tyres both on her left and through Brendan's phone. She then saw a black car with darkened windows as it accelerated away. "Is that you in the car? Where are you going to pick me up from? Where shall I meet you?"

Once his breath had settled he finally responded. "*Meet* me?"

The screams from the foyer grew louder and Vicky stepped away another pace.

Brendan laughed.

"What's so funny?"

"You didn't *seriously* think I was in love with you, did you?"

The words hit Vicky like a gut punch and a shot of acidic bile lifted up her throat. "But ... what?"

"Come on, Vicky, don't be a fucking moron. You were hand selected. We picked you because you were vulnerable. You think it was a coincidence that I was there when you were at your lowest ebb? I didn't have a grandma, you stupid idiot. That was just a ruse to make you trust me. Truth be told, I was waiting for your mum to die so I could be that shoulder to cry on. I made sure I stood next to you in the queue in the hospital's coffee shop for that very reason."

Sweat lifted on Vicky's skin and her breaths grew shallow. "But ... but ..."

"Listen to yourself, will ya? Have some self-respect woman. *Jesus*. Women are so fucking weak. And you know what else?"

So numb she couldn't even cry, Vicky let Brendan continue.

"That night of our first date, the one where you nearly got on the train that blew up. Who do you think blew the train up?"

Vicky gasped as she moved around the side of the Alpha Tower, away from the front door.

"It served two purposes. It killed some of The West's citizens, and it made you believe in fate. We knew you'd be useful once I had your complete trust. It also helped that I wanted to fuck you. You were like my own private whore. Instead of money, I paid you with faux affection. God, you're gullible girl."

Still unable to speak, Vicky held the phone to her ear and stared into space. She heard the screams spill out of the Alpha

Tower. The collective sound of mass panic lit up the air.

"The only advice I have for you now," Brendan said, "is run like the fucking wind. You've helped us turn this virus against your own people. If you want to survive, at least you have a head start on everyone else. At least you know what you're up against. I'll even give you a little hint if you like; there's only going to be one bridge that won't blow up and that's the drawbridge. If you want to get out of the city that's where you need to go."

Vicky heard the screech of tyres from Brendan's side of the phone call.

"I'm crossing it now. Bye, Vicky, it's been emotional."

Vicky let go of her phone and watched it crash to the ground with a *crack*. For a moment, she stood numb with the sounds of insanity just metres away. When a particularly high-pitched scream cut through the madness, she snapped out of her daze and peered around the corner to the front of the Alpha Tower. The carnage of the foyer had already moved outside of the building. She saw blood and open mouths. She heard snarls and roars. She looked across the square. The quickest way to the drawbridge was straight through the middle.

When she glanced down at her phone, she saw the screen had cracked. A picture of her and Brendan stared up from it. Vicky clenched her jaw and crushed the thing beneath her heel.

After one last look at the growing pandemonium, she took a deep breath. The metallic stench of blood filled her sinuses and pushed her tongue up against the roof of her mouth. She half-heaved but managed to cough it away before she ran into the square and in the direction of the drawbridge.

Chapter Nineteen

You only miss a windscreen when you don't have one. Hunched in the front passenger seat, Rhys squinted into the strong wind as he tried to see ahead. The air had cooled to the point where it now burned into his skin. A fly or some other bug tinged against his face every few seconds.

The cold gusts forced Rhys to hold his entire upper body locked tight. He looked across at Larissa who seemed to struggle with the gales as much as he did. He had to shout to be heard over the noise. "Are you okay?"

She looked across, a frown fixed on her face.

Every time Rhys breathed, air rushed into his mouth. "Why don't you slow down a little?"

As if the words gave her the permission she'd sought, Larissa eased off the gas.

Rhys circled his shoulders and rolled his jaw to try to release some of his tension. He then sat up straighter in his seat so he could get a clear look at the front of the car. Only one headlight worked and the bonnet had been dented in several places.

"It's buckled pretty badly, you know."

After Larissa had straightened her back to take a look, she accelerated again and a shudder ran through the car.

Rhys' heart twisted as he watched her pat the steering wheel and say, "Come on, girl, you can keep moving. I trust in you."

The one headlight seemed ineffective against the wall of darkness in front of them. Night closed in from every side as if it would consume the pathetic beam. The wind, although considerably reduced from where Larissa had slowed down, still burned Rhys' eyes as he looked into their inky surroundings. "The fuckers could be anywhere."

"At least we're in a car," Larissa said. "We can outrun them in this if we need to. As long as the roads aren't blocked, we can drive all the way to Biggin Hill Airport."

She'd failed to hide the uncertainty in her words, but neither of them mentioned it. What was the point? If the car broke down, they'd just have to deal with it. A look behind and Rhys saw more darkness. "So they've dropped the virus into London, but where else do you think they've hit?"

Larissa continued to scowl out of the window and Rhys saw her flinch occasionally. The bugs evidently peppered her face like they did his. "How the fuck would *I* know?" she said.

"Hopefully it's much clearer south. I think the worst is behind us."

Even in the face of the wind's onslaught, Larissa dropped her scowl to raise an eyebrow at Rhys.

Okay, so he had no idea how clear the south would be. Another look behind and, other than a faint red glow from their own car's taillights, he saw nothing. "Vicky *will* make it through, you know."

Larissa didn't reply. Instead, she wrung the wheel and stared straight ahead. Even now, after Rhys had spoken to Vicky, the mention of the woman obviously got under Larissa's skin. After a deep breath she finally said, "I *hope* she does." Her voice cracked. "I don't want to live in a world that doesn't have Flynn in it."

"Hey," Rhys said as he reached across and stroked her back, "don't say that."

"But it could happen."

"We can only deal with what we know, and we know Flynn's still alive. Vicky's canny; she'll find a way through. I *know* she'll protect him."

"But you don't even know her, Rhys."

"I know her well enough. You learn a lot about someone when you have to fight for your life next to them."

Another shudder snapped through the car and the vehicle bucked forward.

Rhys looked down at Larissa's feet. "Was that you?"

The car lurched again.

Rhys watched Larissa pump the accelerator, but the car's speed didn't change. A continuous tone then whined from the dashboard and a series of amber, red, and blue lights lit up along it.

Another lurch coughed through the vehicle.

Then the car slowed down.

Unable to penetrate the darkness as he stared into it, Rhys looked for the silhouettes of the diseased nonetheless.

The car continued to lose speed.

"Turn the lights off," Rhys said.

"What?"

"Turn the lights off. If you do that, we'll be able to see our surroundings better. This car hasn't got much left. We need to be ready to get out and we don't want to be attracting attention to ourselves."

Just before Larissa flicked the lights off, Rhys reached into the back seat and retrieved the stool legs. The metal poles, cold to touch, chinked against one another as he pulled them into the front.

The car continued to slow down and more lights popped up on the dash.

After one final lurch, the engine cut out with a *clunk*. The tone that came from the car's dashboard ceased, but the vehicle continued to roll down the road. Rhys listened to the hum of the tyres against the asphalt. The pitch deepened as the car slowed down.

About fifty metres farther along and they'd slowed to a crawl. Rhys sighed. "Just stop the car. We need to get out and walk. At least outside we'll have the room to fight the fuckers."

A gentle squeeze of the brake and Larissa brought the car to a halt. She then popped her seatbelt free.

The lit up dashboard gave a red highlight to her worry lines. The glow would call to the diseased like proverbial moths to a flame. Rhys handed her two of the stool legs. "Come on, we haven't got far to go."

Larissa opened the door and the car's interior light dazzled Rhys. It took him three swipes before he'd managed to flick it off. When they both got out into the quiet night, he whispered to Larissa, "Leave the doors open. The less sound we make the better."

Once out of the car Rhys paused for a moment to let his heart rate settle. When he'd calmed down a little, he listened to the lapping water next to them and the sound of crickets. Summit City still burned on their right and the smell of molten plastic hung heavy in the air. "I think we're ahead of them," Rhys said.

"You said that last time."

He looked to his left at the dark woodland area. A thick wall of black stared back. "I know, but Vicky said the disease got spread by the helicopters. Why would they have gone to Biggin Hill when they had somewhere like London to infect?"

Larissa snorted a laugh. "Biggin Hill's already full of the undead, anyway."

Despite the severity of their situation, Rhys couldn't help but smile. In the few seconds they'd been out of the car, his eyes had already adjusted to the darkness. The moon, although not full, provided enough light for them to see. If a diseased appeared nearby, at least they'd see its silhouette. Better than not being able to see it at all. With Larissa still close to him, he watched her chew her bottom lip as she looked around. "We've come this far," he said. "We'll get all the way."

Larissa didn't look convinced. She then gasped and froze. "Hear that?"

"What?"

She didn't reply and Rhys strained his ears. Although far away, he caught the briefest sound as it rode on the wind. He heard the cries of the diseased. With a quickened pulse and shallow breaths he said, "It must be the mob that's chased us from London. Better behind than in front of us, I suppose."

"It's a small fucking consolation, Rhys. Did you *see* how many there were?" Larissa walked away.

A shudder snapped through Rhys as the image of the shambling horde that raced down the hill came back to him. He heard another call from the diseased and the toxic smell of Summit City took on the slightest vinegar reek of rot. For a moment, he froze and watched the darkness before he spun on his heel and ran after his ex-wife.

Chapter Twenty

About ten hours ago

As Vicky stood in the control booth, sweat coated her entire body. It set her skin alight with itchiness, but she remained still, shocked as she watched Rhys walk back across the drawbridge into the city. When presented with a chance to run for freedom he'd decided to head back into insanity to rescue a woman he hated. Maybe if she had a child she'd understand. By the end of the day, she may have a child; someone would have to look after Flynn if Rhys didn't come back. She could still call after him and refuse to take care of the boy. Sure, he'd hate her, but it would keep him and his son together.

But she didn't move. Instead, she stood there and did fuck all to stop him from throwing his life away.

***

Vicky sank into the seat in the warm car. After the long day, the heat soaked into her sore muscles and her body turned limp. Her eyelids grew heavy and each blink lasted longer than the previous one. With a deep sting in her tired eyes, she looked at the control booth and the surrounding area. No diseased. Another long blink and her eyelids stuck together for a second before she pulled them wide again. She looked up the road that led to Flynn's primary school. It seemed clear.

The diseased on the other side of the river groaned and roared. The background noise of fury had been so consistent that Vicky had almost stopped hearing it. A huge river and raised drawbridge kept them at bay. If the diseased were to come from anywhere, it would be from Flynn's school. But with the heavily populated South London so close, why would they head back toward Summit City?

Vicky straightened her back and rubbed her face. The warm air seemed to stick to her and no matter what she did, she couldn't shake the lethargy it brought with it. When she looked into the back of the car, she saw Flynn curled up and asleep in the foetal position. Were it not for him, she would have been on her way to The Highlands by now. She should have learned from Brendan that she needed to look after herself and not let anyone take advantage of her. Yet here she was again, a sitting duck while some man went off and became a hero. Or, more likely, got himself killed.

The walkie-talkie hissed on the seat next to Vicky and her pulse surged as she looked down at it. She straightened in her seat as Rhys' voice blared out of the small speaker. Clumsy with tiredness, she fumbled for the handset. She finally grabbed it and pressed the talk button down.

"Hi."

"How's my boy doing?"

Flynn opened his eyes on the back seat and Vicky kept her voice low. She turned the volume of the walkie-talkie down by a few notches as she checked her surroundings again. Just because she couldn't see them, that didn't mean they wouldn't hear her. "He's good. We're both good. It's all quiet here. Well, I say quiet but the diseased are still waiting on the other side of the bridge thinking they can get across. Stupid fuckers. Hopefully they'll be gone when you come back. How are things with you?"

When no reply came back Vicky drew a breath to speak again, but Rhys cut her off.

"I'm doing fine. I'm making good progress. Anyway, I don't want to run the battery down. I just needed to check everything's all right. I'll contact you again soon, okay?"

"Okay," Vicky said.

"I love you, Flynn."

The groggy boy on the back seat stretched, sat up, and spoke into the walkie-talkie. "Love you too, Daddy."

The line went dead.

***

Vicky had returned to the control booth to look across the river into the city. As she stood in the smell of stale sweat and flatulence, she watched the large collection of diseased that still remained on the other side. Their numbers had diminished a little. Some of the stupid fuckers seemed to have finally worked out how to identify a lost cause, not many of them, but some.

After she'd glanced around again, Vicky looked at the car. Flynn remained in the back as he had done since they'd been there. The only time he'd gotten out was when he needed to take a leak. They may need to mobilise in an instant so he needed to remain inside the vehicle to avoid any delay.

When the walkie-talkie came to life in her hands, Vicky snapped it up. She spoke into it as she continued to look across the river. "Hello?"

"Hi, how are things?"

Vicky stepped out of the hot booth and hid behind the raised drawbridge. They couldn't cross the river, but best not provoke them anyway. She kept her voice low. "We're all good. You?"

"I'm hanging on. I've met a person who also wants to rescue somebody, so we've teamed up. We're keeping each other alive, although there's something I *don't* trust about him."

"Oh?"

"He knew your name."

Vicky frowned. "*My* name?"

"Yeah. I'm sure I didn't tell it to him, but he knew it all the same."

The thought of Brendan sent a shot of adrenaline through Vicky. "Wh- what's his name?"

"Oscar."

Some of the tension left her body.

"At least that's what he told me it is. The fella's handy in a fight though. He's saved my arse on more than one occasion already. I'd be dead by now if it wasn't for him."

It may not have been Brendan, but he must be connected to him in some way. How else would he know Vicky's name?

"Vicky?"

A shake of her head and she snapped out of her daze. "Yeah,

sorry. I'm *worried* about you, Rhys."

"Don't be, I'm fine. Can I talk to Flynn?"

Vicky crossed the space between her and the car and handed Flynn the walkie-talkie.

The boy pressed the button on the side in. "Hi, Dad."

"Are you okay, mate?"

After he'd nodded several times, Flynn clutched the walkie-talkie with both hands and said, "I'm fine. When are you coming back? Have you found Mummy?"

"I won't be long now. I've spoken to Mummy and she's going to be coming out of the city with me. Just hang on there, yeah?"

"Okay."

"I love you, mate."

"I love you too, Dad."

Vicky took the walkie-talkie back. Oscar had to have something to do with Brendan. "Just be careful, yeah?" she said. If she had said more, it would have looked like she had something to hide. "I'll see you before nine."

After she'd slipped the walkie-talkie into her back pocket, Vicky lost focus as she stared into space.

"They'll be okay, won't they?"

"Huh?"

A watery glaze covered Flynn's eyes as he stared up at her. "Mummy and Daddy. They'll be okay?"

A forced smile and Vicky stroked Flynn's face. "Of course they will. You don't need to worry. Your daddy's a superhero."

***

The *thwip thwip* of a helicopter blade sounded out and Vicky poked her head out of the car's window to look up into the sky behind her.

A large helicopter, military by the look of it, came from the direction of Summit City. It flew so low Vicky felt the vibration from the loud propeller in her chest.

When it got overhead, she saw the large cage beneath it and her toes curled. It had five or six diseased inside. The angry faces of the monsters stared down as they scanned for prey. One of them watched Vicky with its bloody eyes and snapped at the air as if it could taste her.

"What's *that*?" Flynn asked.

Vicky continued to look up as it pulled away. "A helicopter, sweetie."

"Are they here to save us?"

The helicopter headed in the direction of London.

"I don't think so. I think they have other things in mind."

When she looked into her mirror at Flynn behind her, she watched him sink back into his seat. "Maybe they'll come back and pull Mummy and Daddy out of Summit City like they have with those people."

Vicky didn't reply. Instead, she watched the helicopter get smaller as it headed toward London and the cage swung beneath it.

***

Evening had settled in and the temperature had dropped by a few degrees. With the crisper air, Vicky had managed to shake the lethargy from her muscles and she could finally sit in the car without sweating. However, her tacky skin still itched from the day's perspiration and she'd have killed for a shower. When she looked in her rear-view mirror at Flynn, who sat up on the back seat, she smiled and the boy smiled back. He gave her the grin of a child reciprocating a gesture. The deep frown that had been etched on his face for the past few hours remained. A boy that young shouldn't have to deal with this. After a long sigh, Vicky said, "So what do you want to be when you grow up?"

"A fireman."

She laughed. "Wow, you *really* know what you want to be, huh? I admire that, a man who knows who he is and where he's going."

The boy's worried frown shifted to one of confusion.

Vicky drew another deep breath, but before she could speak the walkie-talkie cut in. "Vicky, it's Rhys, come in."

"Rhys?"

"Why would someone from The East know your name? What have you done?"

Ice ran through her veins and her stomach tensed. His question cut straight to the pain of what Brendan had done to her. "I … I don't know, Rhys. I don't know what you're talking about."

"If you don't know what I'm talking about why do you sound so fucking nervous?"

The temperature in the car rose and Vicky didn't reply. When she looked in the rear-view mirror again, she saw fear in Flynn's wide eyes.

"Brendan told me to say *hi*."

A surge of adrenaline ran a violent shake through her limbs

and Vicky dropped the handset into the footwell.

Rhys' voice called up at her. "Vicky? What the fuck's going on? What aren't you telling me?"

After she'd reached down and picked the walkie-talkie up again, she pressed the button on the side. She couldn't lie to him. "I'm sorry, Rhys. I'm truly sorry. If I'd have known it would have come to this, I wouldn't have done *anything*, I *promise*. I'm so, so sorry."

"What have you *done*? *Where's my boy?*"

Vicky looked at Flynn in the mirror.

"*Vicky?*"

The boy chewed on his lip and she shook her head. He didn't need to fear her. Everything would be okay. Vicky turned the walkie-talkie off.

In the silence, Flynn stared at her.

"Everything's going to be okay. Trust me."

But the boy didn't reply. Instead, he looked at the back door to his right as if to work out a route of escape. When he looked back at her, he continued to frown.

***

Despite the conversation Vicky had had with Rhys, Flynn had remained in the car with her. Another glance at the clock in the car's dashboard and she sighed. "We don't have much longer now."

"Much longer until what?" Flynn said.

"Until your mummy and daddy arrive." Maybe she shouldn't get the kid's hopes up, but hope seemed like it would be in very short supply soon so she may as well use it while she still could.

Nighttime had started to tighten its grip on the day as the sun set and the air cooled further. Vicky looked at the little boy who had now moved to the passenger seat next to her. She'd reassured him that he could trust her and told him to come up front. He seemed reluctant at first, but he did as she asked. "In about half an hour your mummy and daddy should be coming across the river." If they didn't, the heat of the incineration would turn them into sludge on the city's streets. She chose to keep that detail to herself.

Before she could say anything else to the boy, a loud *bang* shook through the car. Vicky's heart stopped when she looked in the rear-view mirror and saw Brendan. Wild-eyed and red-faced, he had his hands pressed down against the vehicle's boot and screamed before he ran around to the driver's side door.

"Get out of the car *now*," she said to Flynn.

The boy complied, popped the passenger door open, and fell out onto the road. Before Brendan could open her door, Vicky tore the keys from the ignition and climbed across the car after Flynn. Brendan reached in and grabbed her ankle.

His tight grip stung, but she twisted and shook to try to get free. In the struggle, she bashed the horn. A loud *tooooot* called out into the quiet evening. When she saw the shock on Brendan's face at the sound, she snapped her leg free and pulled far enough away from the lunatic to avoid his axe as he swung it at her. The bloody weapon hit the handbrake with a loud *clang* and chipped a chunk of plastic away from it.

"You ain't getting away, you bitch. Your boyfriend fucked me over and now *you're* going to pay the fucking price for it. You and his horrible little kid."

Fear pulled Vicky's chest tight and she couldn't catch her breath as she scrambled away from Brendan.

Another walkie-talkie rested on the dashboard in front of the passenger seat. When Vicky had tested it earlier, it spoke to the radio inside the vehicle. She grabbed it, and just as Brendan lurched for her again, she fell out of the open passenger door and hit the ground so hard the jolt ran a shock through her left shoulder.

As she got to her feet, she heard the enraged scream of the diseased and froze. They must have heard the horn. Then she saw them. Three diseased, all women, ran at the car from Brendan's side. With the man half in the vehicle, they looked set to end him.

But Brendan pulled himself in and pulled his door closed just before the first one reached him.

Vicky slammed the passenger door shut and leaned against it. Thank God Flynn had closed the window on that side when he'd gotten cold earlier. She'd been tempted to tell him to man up when he did it because the car had been too hot as it was, but it now prevented Brendan from getting through to them.

The *whack* of Brendan's axe hit the other side of the glass. It cracked it, but it didn't break through. The confined space restricted his swing, but the window would only take one more whack at the most. Vicky looked into Flynn's wide eyes. "We're going to run in three seconds, okay?"

The boy trembled but he nodded.

Another *crack* of the axe against the window and Vicky heard the splinter of more glass. One more swing and the axe would be in her back for sure. She nodded at Flynn. "Three … two … one!"

The car shook just before Vicky pulled away from it. As she ran, she turned around to see the first of the diseased had climbed in through the driver's side window to get to Brendan. A flurry of activity, and she lost sight of the big man to the flailing limbs inside the car. The next diseased followed the first inside. Fuck knows why they left her and Flynn alone. Impossible to tell which arm belonged to whom, she looked forward again and followed Flynn. They ran in the direction of the dead police officers. The direction of Flynn's school … The direction of London … Fuck knows what they would find there.

Chapter Twenty-One

The sound of the diseased remained well behind Rhys and Larissa. They couldn't outrun them forever, but maybe they could get to Biggin Hill Airport before the things caught up with them … maybe.

The street, wide and uninhabited, seemed like it could be clear for miles. Although with no more than about twenty metres visibility, Rhys couldn't let the false sense of security relax him. Anything could spring from the dark. "I know I've said it before, but I'd rather have them behind us than in front," Rhys said.

Larissa looked around. "I'd rather they weren't *anywhere*."

With his poles raised, Rhys walked by Larissa's side. Permanently alert, he stared into the grainy darkness. The dense woods ran a border on their left and the glow of the city flanked their right.

Whenever either one of them spoke their voices carried in the quiet night air. If anything waited for them up ahead, they'd hear them all right.

"Rhys?"

"Yeah?"

"What exactly was the helicopter doing? You said they've dropped the virus in London, but you didn't explain any more than that."

Rhys kept his eyes ahead as they walked. "When I was in the city, I saw a helicopter trapping the diseased in a cage and then lifting them out. They baited them with a live human, locked the cage on them, and carried them away. Oscar ... Brendan, or whatever the fuck his name is, told me that The East were airlifting the diseased out and dropping them in the major UK cities. They've even dropped some in mainland Europe. Vicky saw the helicopter too."

"So we're fucked?"

Rhys didn't have an answer for that. After a few seconds, he finally said, "It's best to not think of it like that. Let's just take one step at a time. We need to meet up with Flynn and Vicky and make sure *they're* okay. Once we've achieved that, we can think about what to do next. The possibilities of what *could* happen are too overwhelming to comprehend, but I don't think the virus has spread from the diseased that spilled out of Summit City. I think the disease is coming down from London where The East dropped it, which means—"

"It's behind us," Larissa finished for him, a taut impatience in her tone.

After he'd sighed, Rhys lifted his shoulders in a shrug. "I know that's what I keep saying, but that's what I *hope*."

Superman's glow-in-the-dark arms stared up at Rhys from Flynn's watch. "We have forty-five minutes to get to the airport. We can meet Vicky there and then plan our next step."

"*We?* I hope you're not including Vicky in that *we*."

"Why wouldn't I?"

"Because she can't be trusted?"

"And Oscar's opinion can? I'm reserving judgment on Vicky until I've spoken to her."

"Well, I hope your openness doesn't lead to the death of our son."

"I think Vicky's doing a good job with him so far." The words stuck in his throat and he had to force them out. "Flynn won't die. He *won't*. And Vicky will bring him back to us safe and sound. I think …" Rhys froze. He stared into the dark and listened to the sound of feet approaching from the direction they were heading in.

He then lifted the broken stool legs and squinted to try to see better, but their surroundings were too dark. Although the sound got louder, he saw nothing.

Rhys' raised stool legs trembled in his grip while Larissa stood alert next to him. As the sound drew closer, he swallowed a dry gulp.

The footsteps came at them quicker, a drum roll of a beat. Much faster than they could run, they'd have to stand a fight.

So dark, Rhys dared not blink, his eyes ached from straining them to see something, anything. Still, he saw nothing and the clumsy beat of a diseased's run continued to close in on them.

Suddenly a shadow shot from the darkness and sprinted past them.

So fast Rhys barely had the time to see it.

Once he'd regained his composure, he laughed as the thing disappeared into the darkness. "A dog? Jesus, I thought we were done for then." A second later, he sighed. "Doesn't the poor thing realise it's heading toward a ravenous mob?"

"I think you're asking the wrong question, Rhys."

"Oh?"

"I think you should be asking, *What the fuck is it running from?*"

The hairs lifted on the back of Rhys' neck and his jaw fell loose. What the fuck *was* it running from?

Chapter Twenty-Two

About three hours ago

Once they'd run over the brow of the hill, Vicky looked at the huge highway in front of them. Seven lanes wide on each side of the road, it bottlenecked down into a dual carriageway for the traffic that needed to cross the bridge into the city. Just the thought of rush hour made Vicky tense with a Pavlovian response to something that she'd probably never experience again.

Vicky paused and hunched down as she let her heart rate settle. She pulled on Flynn's arm and he squatted down next to her.

"Imagine we're playing *Call of Duty: Zombies* and we're the snipers," Vicky said. She pretended to talk into a walkie-talkie. "Okay, soldier?"

The wide and glassy eyes of the little boy regarded Vicky before he gulped and nodded at her. "Okay."

Vicky pointed two fingers at her eyes and then pointed them to the brow of the hill back in the direction they'd just come from.

Flynn followed her lead and looked to where she'd pointed.

After she'd patted his back, Vicky pulled the boy's slight frame in close to hers. "Over the other side of that hill are the Nazi zombies. We need to creep close enough to the brow to see over, but we need to make sure the Nazi zombies don't see *us*, okay?"

A half-smile lifted Flynn's pale face.

"You ready, soldier?"

After he'd nodded at her, Flynn threw up a clumsy left-handed salute and said, "Yes, sir."

Vicky lay down on her front against the road surface. The hard asphalt retained the day's warmth. As she commando crawled, the car key in her pocket dug into her right thigh with a sharp sting every time she put pressure on that side. The younger and sprightlier of the two, Flynn kept pace with her with no problem.

When they got close, Vicky stopped and looked at Flynn again. She pushed her finger across her lips and whispered, "You ready for this, solider?"

Wide eyes and tight lips stared back at her, and Flynn nodded.

With a rapid pulse and wobbly limbs, Vicky crawled farther up the hill. When she got close to the top, she lifted her head and peered over. Her heart sank.

The door to the police car hung open and Brendan had gotten to his feet. The diseased in the car writhed and moaned, locked in their perpetual torment, and all still *very* alive.

As Brendan moved off, the diseased continued their pursuit of him. Injured and covered in blood, the creatures slipped from the car like slugs and hit the hard road with wet slaps. Brendan paused to watch them.

Handicapped by the damage he'd dealt to them, each one glistened with blood and reached out to the big man. A gust of wind sent their reek up the hill and an involuntary spasm of revulsion twisted through Vicky's face.

Long bony fingers stretched Brendan's way and they snapped their jaws and snarled. However, with such poor mobility after their fight in the car they had nothing else to attack him with.

Vicky felt Flynn move into her side and the little boy shook violently. Once Brendan had killed the diseased, she'd move on. For some reason his intense fascination with the things kept her in place. Maybe he had no plans to kill the monsters. After all, he wanted the virus to spread.

When Brendan turned away from the diseased, ice gripped Vicky as his cold stare locked onto hers. He was going to leave them alive, she could see it in his eyes. "Come on, Flynn," she said as she jumped to her feet.

"But what about the Nazi zombies?"

Vicky didn't reply. Instead, she watched Brendan as he walked around to the driver's side of the police car and peered through the window.

The key still dug into her thigh, a sharp reminder that unless he hot-wired the car he had no transport.

Brendan looked up at her and his dark eyebrows dipped in a hard frown.

Dizzy from her frantic pulse and frozen to the spot, Vicky pulled Flynn against her and watched the big man. They couldn't outrun him, not with Flynn to take care of. Better to watch Brendan's next move than to try to outpace him. Then she saw it.

Every time he tried to stand on his right leg, he limped. Even the slightest pressure seemed to cause him discomfort. He looked like he could fall over at any moment.

Without a car, the guy had no chance of catching them. Not that she should underestimate Brendan. Even with his injury, she'd just witnessed him handicap three diseased inside a cramped car.

"Come on, Flynn," Vicky said as she tugged on the boy's shoulder. She continued to watch the lunatic man down by the car. "Let's get out of here."

The rage in Brendan's stare cut straight to her core. His hair darkened with blood and the red streaks of it ran down his face. She shouldn't underestimate him at all.

Chapter Twenty-Three

After a couple of seconds, Rhys heard the clumsy slap of feet against concrete. The heavy thuds, much heavier than the dog's had been, but moving at a slower pace, came their way. "They're close," he said. "And it sounds like there's more than one of them."

With both stool legs raised, Larissa widened her stance.

Rhys did the same as he heard to the phlegmy rattle of wet lungs.

Rhys drew deep breaths in a useless attempt to calm his nerves. A flutter of anxiety ran through his entire body and his heavy arms reminded him just how little rest he'd had that day.

The uncoordinated stumble drew closer, but no matter how many times Rhys blinked, he couldn't see any farther ahead.

The rotten smell hit before Rhys saw them. He twisted his face but remained focused in front. It sounded like only a couple of diseased, but he couldn't be sure.

In a flash, a wide mouth, bleeding eyes, and a vicious scream burst from the darkness. With only a second to react, Rhys drove one of the stool legs into its eye. The pole passed straight through its head and popped out of the other side with a small explosion of brain matter and skull.

When Rhys moved aside, the thing continued past him for a few steps before it fell. The pole that still protruded from its face caught on the ground, snapped its head down toward its chest, and flipped the creature over the top of it.

As he watched the diseased slam down hard on the concrete, another scream called out ahead of them.

Two more diseased appeared. Incensed, they flailed in his direction and Rhys had to jump aside again to avoid what seemed like an inevitable collision.

Both diseased ran past him, stopped, turned, and looked back at him.

With Larissa closer to them, Rhys readied his pole to help her out. But they ignored her and came straight at him again. Both of them, as one, seemed intent on ending him where he stood.

Rhys looked from one of his attackers to the other, but before he had to decide which one to fight, Larissa appeared from the side and drove one of her poles through the temple of the one closest to her.

With his focus fully on the other, Rhys speared it like he had the last one and watched it fall.

Rocked by heavy breaths, Rhys looked at the downed diseased. Sprawled out on the ground, all three of them lay dead. A glance at Larissa and he forced a laugh out. "Fuck. Thank you."

Larissa dipped a nod. "You're welcome. Why did they go for *you* and not me?"

"I'm guessing it's the same reason they went for a diseased baby when I threw one."

"You *threw* a *baby*?"

"It's a long story, but basically these creatures feel empathy for one another. I just killed one of their own. I think they wanted to end me before they focused on you."

"So they have empathy for one another, *and* they know how to hunt and survive?"

Numb from the day, Rhys' vision blurred as he looked down at the things. "It doesn't bear thinking about, does it?" He nodded into the darkness in front of them. "Come on, let's get the fuck out of here. We only have about half an hour to get to Biggin Hill."

***

With the smell of the diseased still up his nose, Rhys sniffed to try to clear it. The tang of burned plastic found a way in. A quick glance to either side and Rhys returned his attention to the darkness in front. Maybe they'd just been lucky so far, but it seemed like the woods were too dark even for the diseased. They didn't need them coming out of there too.

"So what does it mean?" Larissa asked.

"Huh?"

"If the diseased can hunt and have empathy for one another, surely that suggests they could form some kind of community?"

"Well, they hunt in packs already, but I doubt they'll start building houses and shit. I can't see their town meetings being that fun." Rhys laughed. Larissa didn't.

"They seem to have a pack mentality," Rhys continued, "but

I don't know if they're any more cognitive than, I dunno, a herd of cows or something."

Rhys watched Larissa scratch her face as she frowned into the darkness. She then ran a hand through her short black hair. "I hope they don't evolve."

Rhys shook his head. "I don't even want to think about that."

Larissa didn't reply.

Only a few sounds made it through the near silence around them: the scrapes of their feet over the concrete road surface, the occasional cough from Larissa, a barking dog, and behind them …

"I think they'll outlive us, you know," Larissa said. "I think they'll have the run of this world and there's fuck all we can do about it."

"With how quickly the disease spreads," Rhys said, "you may just be right. Maybe Homo sapiens will become nothing but a memory as a new superhuman takes over. The ultimate killing machine, maybe they will outlive us … although, there has to be some chinless wonder somewhere with their pudgy finger on the big red button."

"Big red button?"

"Nuclear war. With the way we've worked as a species, we'll make sure we destroy the planet rather than move on quietly. We don't have it in us to accept a world that isn't being destroyed by humans."

"That's bleak."

"Yeah, but look at what we've just released into the world. We're a parasite on this earth and the planet would be better without us."

In the silence that followed, Rhys tuned into the background noise of their pursuers. With every minute that passed, they grew louder. Another glance at Flynn's Superman watch and he sped up a little. "We've gotta pick up the pace, 'Rissa. We only have about twenty minutes to get to Biggin Hill … and we need to make sure we outrun those fuckers behind," he said. "They catch up with us and we're fucked."

Chapter Twenty-Four

About three hours ago

"Where are we going?" Flynn asked.

After she'd glanced behind to the brow of the hill, Vicky pulled on Flynn's small hand and said, "Away from here."

The boy moved along with her, but his clear reluctance dragged him back a little.

Vicky looked behind again before she returned her focus to the boy. "Just remember *Call of Duty: Zombies*, okay?"

A confused frown crushed his small face and Flynn looked behind too.

"I can't believe they're still making them," Vicky said to try and jolly him along. "I used to play those games when *I* was a kid." As hard as she tried, she struggled to keep the panic from her voice, and from the way Flynn looked at her, she could see that he felt it too.

Breathless from keeping up with Vicky's pace, Flynn nodded. "They're on number forty-two now."

Brendan still hadn't appeared over the brow of the hill. "The only difference between the game and what's happening now," Vicky said, "is that we don't have guns, so we *have* to run instead of fight."

"Okay." Flynn looked behind again and picked up his pace.

"We need to pretend the man that tried to get into the car is a zombie. He moves like them, all slow and shuffling."

Although Flynn replied, Vicky didn't hear him because she saw Brendan at that moment. The pain of the grief she'd not yet been allowed to feel ripped through her as if her insides had been torn. She stared at his chiselled face and dark hair, darker than usual from being soaked in blood. Streaks of it ran down his pale features and dripped off his strong jaw line. He glared at her through wild and wide eyes. The ice blue of his irises used to comfort her; now they sent a chill to her core as she felt the cold focus of a psychopath.

When she looked down at Flynn next to her, she saw him look back at their pursuer.

The grimace on Brendan's face spoke of his pain. "As long as we can keep moving," Vicky said loud enough for Brendan to hear, "the stupid zombie won't be able to catch us."

The grimace of pain turned to one of rage and fierce determination as Brendan limped after them. But as Vicky locked eyes with him, they both knew the truth of it. This once perfect physical specimen of a man had nothing left to give; a six year old and a woman had him beat.

A check of her watch and Vicky looked across at the city on their left. In fifteen minutes it would be aflame with Rhys and Larissa still inside.

***

Like something from a ridiculous comedy film, Vicky, handicapped by Flynn's small legs, moved as quickly as she could, and Brendan hobbled after them. They'd tried a short sprint, but Flynn gassed out and needed to rest. It made them slower than before.

The pavement along the side of the road went uphill and turned into a footbridge that gave pedestrians a way to cross the busy and wide highway should they need it. Not that it served any purpose at this time of night. The road, free of homes and shops, stood abandoned outside of rush hour.

With their elevated view, Vicky could see Summit City more clearly. Five minutes until the place went up in flames. She pulled the police car's walkie-talkie from her pocket and continued to tug Flynn along behind her. The second she turned it on, Rhys' voice crackled through the small speaker. "Hello."

Vicky panted when she said, "Rhys, it's me. I've fucked up big time, but you *can* trust me. Please believe me when I say that." Panic stole her breath more than the physical exercise so she stopped to recover. Flynn looked glad for the rest too as the boy hunched over and caught his breath.

"Where's Flynn?" Rhys said.

"With me. He's okay." Vicky watched Brendan step onto the footbridge about one hundred metres behind them. The incline slowed him down.

"Where are you?"

"I had to move."

"Where are you?"

Brendan shouted up at Vicky, "Come here, you *bitch*."

Flynn's tiny hand squeezed Vicky's and he said, "I'm *scared*. Where are we going? I want my mum and dad."

"Vicky," Rhys said. "Where are you? What's happening?"

Adrenaline and exhaustion combined to shake Vicky's hand so badly she dropped the walkie-talkie. Before she could grab it, the thing bounced across the walkway and fell down to the road below. It hit the hard ground with a sharp *crack* and pieces of plastic exploded away from it. After she'd looked back at Brendan, Vicky's heart sank. She saw Flynn look down at it. "We've got to leave it, buddy. If we stop to get it then the Call of Duty zombie will catch us. Besides, there ain't no fixing it."

After he'd looked down at it again, Flynn looked up at Vicky.

"If I put you on my shoulders, can you hold on?"

Flynn nodded. "Clive used to do that with me all the time."

"Okay." Vicky lifted the boy up and over her head. A heavy pressure on the back of her neck, she looked behind at Brendan again before she moved off over to the other side of the road at a jog.

***

It wouldn't do any good to tell him not to look. As a boy of this new world, he had to desensitise quick. Before Flynn could say anything, Vicky squeezed his shins. "Bad people did this to the police."

The scene seemed unchanged from when she'd been there with Rhys on their way to rescue Flynn. A burned out car and executed police officers. Nothing but corpses and carnage.

The dampness of urine soaked the back of Vicky's neck and ran down through her shoulder blades. It made her entire back tense and she shuddered. The urge to throw the boy to the ground coursed through her, but she resisted. Then she saw it and her attention left her piss-soaked shirt.

A heave lifted up inside of her when she looked at the police officer. The woman lay on the ground much like the others who'd been executed, but this woman had something different about her. A red soupy mess sat where her stomach should have been. It glistened in the fading light and Vicky saw teeth marks in her flesh where she'd had chunks taken from her. But she had a bullet wound in her forehead like the others, so whatever had done this had done it after the woman had died. It had feasted on her.

Sweat stood out on Vicky's brow and her stomach turned again. "Keep looking straight ahead," she called up to Flynn and felt him snap his view straight. "I need you as a lookout up there, soldier, you got that?"

"Yes, sir."

Maybe he didn't need to desensitise right at that moment.

They passed another couple of police officers who hadn't been eaten. To bend down ran deep pains through Vicky's already tired legs, but she did it anyway and retrieved a baton from each one's belt. Only about six inches long, most people wouldn't recognise them for what they were. She snapped the first one away from her and the telescopic pole popped out to over a foot in length. She lifted it up to Flynn and said, "Here, take this, you may need to use it. I know they're only batons, but the zombies will still fall if we whack them with them, especially the big one on our tail."

After Flynn had taken it, she snapped one open for herself.

Just before they moved off again, a loud *whoosh* sounded out that turned their surroundings from night to day as Summit City lit up like the sun. A ball of heat swelled outwards and blew Vicky's hair back. "Good job your mum and dad got out, eh?"

Flynn didn't reply.

For a second or two Vicky watched the tall flames claw at the huge towers. She then moved off again. With Brendan on their tail, they had to keep going.

***

About half an hour had passed and they hadn't seen Brendan for at least twenty minutes. They'd finally arrived at the town she drove past with Rhys when they'd gone to rescue Flynn. The first house, still about fifty metres away, had a white garage door with blood sprayed up it. When she'd seen it previously with Rhys, the dark stain told them the virus had gotten out and gotten ahead of them. Vicky stared at it and silence hung in the air like low-lying fog.

Vicky lifted Flynn from her shoulders and rolled them to relieve the deep aches she'd gained from carrying the boy. She hunched down to be at his eye level. "You need to walk now, mate. I don't know if any of the diseased are still here or not, but I need to be ready to fight. Besides, I can't carry you anymore. Keep your eyes peeled, solider, and if you see anything, let me know immediately, yeah?"

Flynn blinked several times before he nodded at Vicky. "Okay."

The pair set off again and passed a sign that read 'Welcome to Springfield'.

Just after they'd crossed into the town, the sound of clumsy footsteps pattered against the ground and Vicky's senses all snapped to high alert. She didn't say a word as she pulled Flynn behind her and raised her baton ready for the onslaught. To see Flynn do the same stabbed into her heart. No six-year-old should have to fight for his life.

Two diseased appeared seconds later. The one at the front far outpaced the one behind. Both yelled and screamed and both wore the same masks of ultimate aggression. The one at the front was clumsy but fast. The one behind hobbled as if it carried an injury.

"Stay behind me," Vicky said as she watched their attackers approach.

A deep breath and she met the first diseased with a full swing to the face. The weighty baton caught the monster in the cheek and Vicky felt the end of her weapon sink into it with a textured *crunch*. The monster's head snapped to the side, blood sprayed away from its mouth, and it fell to the ground. Vicky glanced at the second diseased to see about ten metres separated them. It gave her time to swing for the head of the one she'd already knocked down. She felt its skull give in to her heavy blow.

When she stood up, the second monster had caught up to her. It reached out and she had to dodge out of its way.

The thing changed its course and went for Flynn.

"*No!*" Vicky shouted and her loud call echoed through the town. She lurched at the thing and swung hard for its head before it could get to the boy. She caught its temple and the creature's legs buckled beneath it. Like the first, Vicky made sure and buried her baton into its fragile skull.

Heavy pants ran through her as she stared at the two diseased and listened out for more.

Nothing.

The two monsters, both men aged anywhere between twenty-five and forty years old, lay executed in the wooded area at the side of the road. Dark blood, almost black like tar, ran from the wounds in the sides of their heads and pooled on the ground. Vicky hunched down next to one and slipped her hand into its pocket. She found what she was looking for on the first try. "Bingo!"

Dumbstruck, Flynn simply stared at her and shook when she lifted the car key up for him to see. She pressed the unlock button on the key and an orange glow came from a car three houses down.

"Yes," Vicky said and ruffled Flynn's hair. "Let's get the fuck out of here."

***

Before Vicky left, she found a phone in the other man's pocket. It had a sticker across the back of it with the phone's number printed on it. "Must be a work phone," she said to Flynn as she showed it to him. "Why else would someone have their number on the back?"

Flynn shrugged, clearly still too shocked to speak.

"What that means for us is that we can use it. Sure, we can't make any calls from it because we can't unlock it, but we can receive them."

A spade lay on the front lawn of one of the houses next to a mound of earth. "Stay there," Vicky said and jogged over to retrieve it.

After Vicky had folded up her telescopic baton and slipped it into her pocket, she picked the spade up and marched back over toward Flynn. "Look away, son, you don't want to see this."

When Flynn closed his eyes and looked down at the ground, Vicky lifted the shovel and drove it into the forearm of one of the diseased. Sparks flew up and a loud *ching* rang out from where the head of the spade ran straight through the dead creature's arm and hit a rock beneath it. Vicky's hands buzzed from the shock that ran up the handle.

The sound of the spade ran through Vicky's mind for longer than it called out in the quiet street. Tense, her skin tingling as she stood alert, Vicky looked around, squinting as she studied the shadows. She hadn't attracted any unwanted attention. Vicky then placed the spade on the ground and lifted the severed arm. Heavier than she expected it to be, she walked over to the first house with Flynn by her side. When they reached the white garage door, she handed Flynn the phone and said, "Read the number out to me, will ya?"

***

Once they'd finished, Vicky took the phone from Flynn to check she had the number correct. She then tossed the arm aside and pulled the boy close to her. "You've been so brave. Your mummy and daddy will be so proud to hear how well you've done." She then pulled the police car's key from her right pocket and tossed it into a bush at the side of the garage. "No need for that now."

Although silence surrounded them still, a different sensation shimmied through Vicky's skin now she'd gotten closer to a house. With the power in the street out, the windows on every property sat dark and impenetrable. Someone, or some*thing* had to be watching them at that moment.

One final look up and down the road and Vicky shuddered before she finally said, "Come on, let's get out of here."

***

Once inside the car, Vicky smelled the reek of rot from the diseased. Coated in blood, she wound the windows down, but it didn't help remove the heavy stench. She reversed off the driveway so the car faced toward London. Rhys knew of her plan to go to The Highlands so she needed to stick with it. If she didn't, Flynn may never see his parents again.

The car's brake lights lit up the street behind Vicky, and when she looked in her rear-view mirror, she nearly lost her bladder.

Brendan, still with his limp and still with his focused look of hate, shambled up the road behind her.

Without another word so as not to traumatise Flynn any further, Vicky slipped the car into gear with a shaky hand and drove off.

Chapter Twenty-Five

Rhys' eyes itched as he strained to see into the darkness. No matter how many times he blinked or rubbed his eyes, the pitch of night prevented any more than about five metres vision in any direction. Aches streaked up and down his tired legs and sweat stood out on his brow. A sticky film of dirt covered his entire body that pulled his shirt and trousers against his skin.

Rhys fought for breath as he ran and his tired feet slapped down against the hard road. From the sound of Larissa's own heavy steps, she seemed as exhausted as him.

Despite the diseased behind them, Rhys slowed to a walk.

After she'd glanced across at him, Larissa did the same.

Hopefully they had enough of a lead on the mob to get to Biggin Hill Airport before they caught up to them.

Summit City gave off an orange hue like a smouldering bonfire. All of the tall flames had gone, but the place looked like it still burned hotter than hell and the roads looked as if they could melt glass. The plastic reek of the city burned as strong as ever, and after a particularly deep breath, Rhys tasted the chemical funk of it. Although this time, the smell seemed a little different. It had an undertone of singed hair and overcooked sweet meat.

After another glance behind Rhys looked in front again. The sound of the diseased had grown louder, a thunder of clumsy footsteps, but he still couldn't see a thing. By the time he could it would be far too late. Despite his will to run again, his leaden body didn't have it in it.

Larissa looked over her shoulder and stumbled. Once she'd recovered she said, "Do you think they can smell us?"

"No."

"Oh?"

A shake of his head and Rhys elaborated. "When I was in the city, I hid from them on several occasions. If they were able to smell, they would have found us at that point. They were so close it would have been almost impossible to miss us. I think they're a hungry mob on their way south. Sure, they saw us back there and gave chase, but I don't think they know where we are. They'll just keep moving until they find something. It seems to be what they do."

When Larissa didn't reply Rhys looked first at her, and then followed her line of sight.

"One mile," she said as she looked at the sign. "One mile to Biggin Hill Airport."

Silence.

"What if she's not there, Rhys?"

"She *will* be. She'll be there with Flynn. I trust her."

"*I* don't!"

"I know, but it'll be fine. If you don't trust her, trust me when I say everything will work out." Although he encouraged

Larissa to have faith, an anxious pang twisted through him. So many things could go wrong in Vicky's attempts to reunite him with his boy. She would try her hardest, but that didn't guarantee a thing.

The conversation with Larissa had died so Rhys looked again at the burning city. A lump rose in his throat. "I miss Dave."

The scowl lifted from Larissa's face when she looked over at him. Genuine concern softened her eyes. "It's shit how many people have been lost and how many more will go."

After a heavy sigh, Rhys looked up ahead into the darkness again. "Yeah. He didn't deserve to die." Both the grief and the constant need to move robbed his strength and he focused on his breathing again before he finally said, "No one did. I don't know what I'll do without him." Tears blurred his vision. "As much as he used to drive me nuts he also kept me going most days. He gave me an excuse to be angry at someone, but he never took it personally. He could see how much being away from Flynn hurt me."

Larissa dropped her head but didn't reply. Her dark bob fell forward and swayed with her quick steps.

"He listened when I talked about Flynn, and he always wanted me to see him when I drove past his school in the morning."

Larissa flicked her head up and looked at him, her green eyes wide as she said, "You drove past his school?"

"Every day."

"Why?"

Rhys coughed several times and swallowed against the burn in his throat. "I just wanted to see him. An occasional glance at my boy would be enough to keep me going."

For a moment, Larissa didn't respond. A deep inhale and she finally turned back and looked at Rhys. A softness sat in her emerald eyes that he hadn't seen from her in a long time. The tight resentment that pulled crow's feet to her temples had vanished. "I'm sorry. I've put you through a lot of shit and deprived Flynn of the opportunity to have a dad in his life who loves him. I just felt so angry."

It felt natural to reach across so Rhys grabbed Larissa's warm hand as they walked. A wall of ice had separated the pair for years. In that moment, it melted and took Rhys back to a different time, a time when they were happy. The memory of one particular day flooded his mind. "Do you remember when you were pregnant with Flynn?"

Although she didn't look at him, Larissa nodded. "Of *course*."

"Do you remember that day in April? It was super hot and we went to the park for a walk and to buy ice cream."

When he looked at her, Rhys saw the slightest smile on Larissa's face. "Yeah I do. I was like a beached whale then and the heat killed me. But I remember we lay on the grass and talked about the future."

The memory of that day had run through Rhys' head again and again. "It all seemed so simple then. So perfect. So fucking *hopeful*. We would be the best parents and raise our child to be a genius and a well-balanced individual." The sadness he usually felt when he talked about Flynn welled up inside of him.

"And *I* stopped that happening."

Rhys frowned and looked across at her. "Huh?"

"Regardless of what went on between us … of how much you fucked up, Flynn still needed his dad in his life and *I* stood in the way of that."

The fast walk and warm evening made Rhys' palm sweat, but he kept a hold of Larissa's hand and squeezed it. "And I'm sorry that I hurt you."

The mention of what he'd done seemed to stir up fire in Larissa who frowned again before she visibly let it go. "It's in the past. How about we draw a line under it? We're going to need each other now."

Before Rhys could respond she said, "We never let Flynn forget who his Daddy was. Or should I say, Clive never let Flynn forget. Other than the photo by his bedside, Clive would talk about you to Flynn *all* the time. He believed a boy should see his father as a superhero regardless of what had happened. He felt that Flynn should be allowed to make the choice, not us. I even fought Clive about it sometimes. I was hurting so bad and I hated hearing your name. But he always stood up for you even though he knew I'd never feel the way for him that I did for you."

Rhys gasped. *Did she just …?*

"And you know what?" When she looked at him, her eyes were glazed with tears. "Flynn's still young enough to think that of you."

Their dark surroundings became even harder for Rhys to see through his tears. He swallowed several times against the burn in his throat and said, "Things *will* be different now, I promise. I'll be there for Flynn and we'll get him back." Rhys thought about the kiss with Vicky. Sure, she was hot, but it couldn't be any more than a kiss. Flynn didn't need to see his dad with another woman, even if he didn't plan on a relationship with Larissa.

The conversation had taken Rhys' attention away from the noises behind. When he tuned into them they sounded twice as loud as before. After a look over his shoulder, he squeezed Larissa's hand again. "Come on. We need to speed up."

Chapter Twenty-Six

About an hour ago

A loud *bang* coincided with a huge jolt that snapped through the steering wheel and up Vicky's arms. She hadn't seen the diseased until that moment. It had come at them from the dark to their right. Flynn screamed next to her, his voice so shrill it hurt her ears. Driven by instinct more than conscious thought, Vicky moved to one side as the body of the thing flew over the bonnet. It connected with the windscreen with a wet *crunch* and cracks spread away from the point of impact on the glass. When Vicky looked in her rear-view mirror—short of breath from the shock—she saw the broken body of the diseased land on the hard road behind the car like a rag doll.

The sound of Flynn's rapid breaths next to her made Vicky turn to the boy. When she reached across to hold his arm, he flinched and withdrew from her touch. "It's okay, Flynn. They're diseased; we can't think of them as people anymore." Another glance behind and she lowered her voice as she loosened her vice-like grip on the steering wheel. "We can't afford to."

Flynn shook and shivered. Panic still had a tight hold on him and he seemed unable to hear Vicky's words. As a way to get through to him, she drew a deep and loud breath, which swelled her stomach. She then exhaled slowly.

After she'd done it several times, she noticed Flynn's breaths had also slowed a little. Another glance across and she saw how the car's dim interior lights glistened off his sweaty face. Wide-eyed and pale, the boy looked like he'd calmed down slightly, but he still stared ahead as if lost in shock.

When her own heart settled, Vicky checked behind again.

Bright headlights suddenly popped from the darkness and filled the rear-view mirror. Vicky swerved in the road and a loud *thud* ran through the car as she mounted the curb. The shock jolted the wheel again and it stung her wrists. She wrestled the car off the pavement with another *clunk.*

The lights had come from nowhere. One minute she saw the diseased, broken as it lay on the road, the next, full beams stung her eyes.

Flynn looked over his shoulder out of the back window. "Who's *that*?"

"I would imagine it's the man who was following us earlier."

"The zombie man?"

Vicky squinted as she looked into the rear-view mirror again. He'd left his full beam on. It took a few deep breaths before her heart had settled enough for her to reply. "Yeah."

They'd now completely left the area that surrounded Summit City and had entered one of the first suburbs closest to it. Every house, although detached and big enough to have at least four bedrooms, looked the same as the next one. No personality whatsoever, the place looked like it belonged on an American television show about bored housewives. At least they'd gotten off the straight road that led away from Summit City. It would be easier to lose a tail in the tight streets.

Despite hitting the curb, the car still drove straight and everything held together ... for the time being at least. Another glance behind and Vicky looked at the boy next to her again. "It's going to be a wild ride from now on. I need you to hold on and be brave."

Vicky saw him nod in her peripheral vision as she looked ahead again and put her foot down. She reached up and switched the mirror to anti-glare as she pressed the accelerator even harder.

The diluted version of Brendan's headlights remained on her tail. If anything, they got closer.

All four wheels screeched when Vicky threw the car through a chicane. Flynn hit the passenger door with a *whack*. Without a child safety seat, the seatbelt would prove ineffective should they crash and it could kill the boy. She couldn't think of that. If they didn't get away from Brendan, he *would* kill them. Another check behind showed Brendan as close as ever, so close in fact, she couldn't see the bottom of his headlights anymore.

When they passed beneath a streetlight, Vicky looked behind to see the car Brendan had taken. Some kind of sports car; it was red, loud, and unmistakably fast. No way could they outrun him. They'd have to outsmart him.

A glance down at the speedometer and it showed eighty-three miles per hour. The picket fences and driveways flashed past on either side and she could see Flynn as he sat tense and gripped onto his seat.

Their car jolted forward with a *crunch* as the sports car rear-ended them. Vicky looked to see Brendan as he leaned close to his windscreen. Wild-eyed; his teeth showed from where he clenched his jaw. This would only end when one of them was dead.

The road forked up ahead so Vicky eased off. Not much, just by a few miles per hour so she could draw Brendan in closer. He nudged the back of their car again.

Just before he crashed into them for a third time, Vicky threw the car left at the last moment. Again, all of the wheels shrieked and the car slid. When she looked across to the right, she saw Brendan fly off in the other direction. His brake lights punched through the darkness a second later.

The mazy estate had plenty of turns so Vicky took one after the other. The muscles in her arms ached as she negotiated the rat run at high speed. The more complex she could make the route the more likely Brendan would never find them.

When she turned down a dead end road Vicky raced to the end of it, turned the car around, and parked up in a line of other stationary vehicles.

With the engine off, she listened to Flynn on the verge of a panic attack. Vicky unclipped his seatbelt and pulled him over so he could sit on her lap. The poor kid shook and cried in her arms. Vicky rocked him back and forth and kissed the back of his head. The sweaty child smelled sweet like a biscuit. "There, there. It's okay, Flynn. Everything's going to be okay. We've lost the horrible man now." The boy's breaths slowed down a little.

About a minute later, Brendan's sports car shot straight past the end of the road.

Not that anyone would hear them but Vicky spoke in a whisper anyway. "We'll sit here for a short while. We need to wait for the horrible man to be long gone."

***

When the clock in the car's dashboard clicked onto ten forty-five, Vicky lifted Flynn back into his seat. Ten minutes had passed since Brendan had shot across the end of their road. "Strap up. We've left it long enough now. Let's go."

Vicky started the engine and turned the lights on. She pulled out and drove up to the end of the road. When Brendan had shot past, his car had headed left, so she turned right. Although residential, the wide roads allowed her to put her foot down again and the car picked up to sixty miles per hour with ease. Other than a slight wobble in the steering wheel, the car showed no signs of damage from where she'd curbed it.

As she tore through the streets, Vicky couldn't help but notice the darkness of all of the houses. The occasional streetlight remained on but most of them had been switched off too. Although the estate seemed abandoned, a power cut had to be a more reasonable explanation. How many people were currently asleep in their houses with no idea about what came their way?

When she rounded the next bend, she slammed her brakes on and the car screeched to a halt. As she stared up the road, her stomach lurched and forced bile up into her throat.

Chapter Twenty-Seven

With heavy gasps between words Rhys said, "I'm worried … we won't … beat them … to the airport."

After she'd looked behind, Larissa looked at Rhys. The small amount of light cast from the slim moon bounced off her sweaty face. "I agree … I don't think we can beat them."

The slaps of Rhys' and Larissa's feet against the hard road called out across the wide-open space. Each heavy footfall jarred Rhys' entire body. With every minute that passed, the sound of the diseased behind them grew louder. After he'd looked at the dark woods on their left again, the trees so densely packed, the place feasted on even the idea of light, Rhys said, "I need to know how close they are."

When he ran for the woods, Larissa called after him, "Where are you *going*?"

Exhaustion had turned Rhys' legs bandy and nausea boiled in his guts, but he pushed on. He had to know.

By the time he got to the first tree at the edge of the woodland, his face burned and sweat ran into his eyes. When he saw Larissa had chosen to wait for him, her hands on her hips and anxious glances back the way they'd come from, he reached out for a low branch and pulled himself up.

Every second counted so Rhys climbed higher. Each time he pushed off with his legs they wobbled and shook, but he had to keep going.

Blinded by the dark and surrounded by the dusty smell of sap, Rhys boosted himself up too quickly and smashed his head against a branch above him. His entire world spun and he lost his legs. As he fell away from the tree, he reached up and caught a branch.

For a second he held on tight as his pulse pounded. His chest heaved as he fought to breathe and he inhaled the thick reek of the tree.

He may have stayed there for longer—God knows he needed the rest—but the roars of the diseased called out to him. A shake of his head banished the dizziness enough for him to push on.

Of course, both he and Larissa could have climbed a tree to avoid the diseased but that wouldn't get them to Biggin Hill. If the diseased worked out where they were, they could end up in a tree for days. Hell, with the amount of the horrible fuckers on their tail they could be there for days even if they hadn't been seen. It could take an age for the crowd to thin. If they were to get to Flynn, they needed to keep moving and they needed to stay ahead.

After Rhys had climbed another few branches higher the density of the tree thinned and the moonlight cut a slight path through the darkness. With the top of the tree almost within reach, he pushed on.

The next branch Rhys stood on bowed beneath his weight

and he instantly jumped back. He'd climbed high enough. When he looked down to see Larissa, his stomach lurched and he only saw darkness. Hopefully she hadn't moved on without him.

The call of the diseased had grown louder still. He should have just kept going. Why did he think climbing a tree would be a good idea? It was like his five-year-old self had taken control of his senses when he'd been on the ground.

For most of the climb, the woody smell of tree filled Rhys' sinuses but then he caught a whiff of something else. Maybe not even something else, maybe the same woody, dusty smell of his surroundings but soured slightly. Another sniff and he caught it again. The slight rotten vinegar kick of the diseased had a way of curdling every scent, almost as if their festering wounds permeated their surroundings.

Reluctance tugged on his limbs, but now that Rhys had climbed this high, he had to see. He reached out and pulled a couple of branches aside. He saw the road behind them and the sight damn near ripped his stomach out. His dizziness returned with a vengeance and he lost the strength in his legs again.

Chapter Twenty-Eight

About forty minutes ago

The mob of diseased, at least two hundred members deep, paused and stared at Vicky and Flynn. Vicky wrung the steering wheel and her pulse hammered when they screamed. Seconds later, they rushed toward them. "Oh fuck."

After she'd thrown the car into reverse, Vicky headed back the way they'd come from. The car shook and wobbled as she reversed at high speed. Maybe she'd done more damage when she'd hit the curb than she first thought. Hopefully the car would hold together long enough for them to get away.

When the road widened she yanked the wheel left until it locked. The front end of the car swung and the tyres screeched as the vehicle whipped around one hundred and eighty degrees.

Vicky's hand shook as she fumbled with the gear stick and shifted the car into first. The car's wheels spun as she accelerated away back in the direction they'd come from.

When they came to the dead end road on their left that they'd hidden down earlier, Vicky almost went past it. But at the last minute, she hit the brake and turned hard into it. The sudden drop in sped shot Flynn forward in his seat and he hit the dashboard with a *crack*. The boy held his head but he seemed okay.

Vicky returned her attention to the road ahead and the wall at the end of it. It didn't matter where she went because London had fallen. The helicopter that had dropped the diseased had without a doubt succeeded in infecting the place. Her only hope would be to lure the monsters after her and then give them the slip.

When she looked in her mirror, she saw the first of the diseased appear at a full sprint behind her.

With the wall directly in front of them, Vicky accelerated down the quiet street. She watched the tachometer redline but did nothing to change it.

When she got close to the end of the road, she turned a sharp right and pulled the handbrake up. With sweaty and aching hands, she had to hold on extra tight so as not to lose control of the car. The tyres skidded as the car snapped sideways and crashed into the wall at the end with a *crunch*. The impact ran a violent snap through her body and shook Flynn in his seat, but the wall held. It left Flynn unable to get out of his side of the car.

Vicky popped her seatbelt free and held her hand out to the boy. "Come on, we need to go."

As Flynn hopped over, Vicky popped the door open and kicked it wide. The screams and roars of the diseased sounded twice as loud.

Once outside the car, Vicky lifted Flynn onto the roof. The

thunder of hundreds of feet hammered a war cry that descended on them. Their roars damn near deafened Vicky.

Vicky had to shout to be heard. She pointed at the wall she'd wedged the car up against. "You need to climb over that now. I'm coming straight after you."

So close she could smell their rotten stench, Vicky turned around to look at the wall of insanity as it bore down on them. Open mouths, bloody eyes, flailing arms. She stepped onto the car's wing mirror and boosted herself onto the roof as she watched Flynn disappear over the wall.

Once on top of the car, she peered over to find Flynn. He'd gripped onto the top of the wall but hadn't let go. With no more than a metre drop, Vicky looked back at the diseased before she turned on him again. "Let go, Flynn."

"No, I can't."

"Let go. If you don't I can't climb over."

Another shake of his head and Flynn stared at Vicky.

She grabbed both of his wrists and pulled him away from the wall. She then lowered him down until he had about half a metre drop. When she let him go, he screamed.

The first of the diseased crashed into the side of the car with a loud *boom* and the vehicle shook beneath Vicky's feet. A second later and they'd swarmed around it. The car shook some more as they bashed and thumped it. Vicky hopped up and straddled the wall.

Just before she lifted her leg over the other side, she heard the screech of car tyres. A glance up the road and exhaustion overwhelmed her when she saw the flame-red sports car.

The diseased crammed the street but Brendan drove through

them regardless. The man obviously cared more about revenge than he did his own well-being. Some moved but it still sounded like the man had hit a line of cones when Vicky heard the *thud, thud, thud,* of diseased bodies meeting the car's bumper.

Vicky nearly pissed herself when she locked eyes with the crazed Brendan. Just before he got to the end of the road, she lifted her leg over the wall and dropped down onto the other side.

Flynn had waited for her. The street on this side seemed quiet.

A *crash* sounded. Brendan must have driven straight into Vicky's car.

When Vicky heard the car door open on the other side of the wall, she tugged on Flynn's hand. "Come on, let's go."

The pair ran away.

***

The virus seemed to have spread to most of the suburb's residents already. To try to outrun it would be madness so Vicky looked for somewhere to hide.

At that moment, the phone Vicky had taken from the diseased in the last town rang. She grabbed Flynn's small hand and darted down an alleyway. After she'd pressed the answer button, she fought to level her breath and said, "Hello."

"Vicky? Where the fuck are you?" Rhys said.

She lowered her voice and gasped. "I'm *trying* to get away from Brendan. I can't see him, but he hasn't given up on our trail. The guy's a *psychopath*."

The diseased on the other side of the wall roared. Hopefully they had Brendan.

"Is it bad where you are too?"

For a moment, Vicky didn't reply. She finally said, "London's fallen, Rhys. It's fucked. When I was waiting for you in the police car, I saw a helicopter fly over with a cage of those creatures. I think they've dropped the disease onto it. Flynn and I have to turn around and head back toward Summit City."

"Flynn's okay, is he?"

After she looked at the shocked and dishevelled boy Vicky said, "He's fine."

Vicky heard Larissa in the background. "Let me speak to him."

"Focus on driving, Larissa," Rhys replied. "Vicky, we need to think of somewhere we can meet."

"I agree. We need to go south too because there's nothing left of London." She listened to the diseased and moved off again down the tight alleyway. "How about Biggin Hill Airport?" Vicky said. "There's an old industrial estate next to it. I can't imagine there'll be many of the diseased there."

More screams sounded out behind Vicky, and when she rounded the next corner, her entire body sank at the sight of yet another dead end.

"Okay," Rhys said. "We can get to Biggin Hill Airport. Can you meet us there in an hour?"

Vicky looked at the tall brick wall that barred their way and tried to keep the sound of panic from her voice when she finally said. "Yes, I can."

"Can we speak to Flynn?"

Vicky continued to watch the wall as she handed the phone to Flynn.

"Dad?"

His shrill voice called out in the night and Vicky nearly snatched the phone away from him. Instead, she pressed her finger into her lips and glared at the boy.

Flynn lowered his voice to a whisper. "I'm *scared*, Dad."

The boy listened into the phone for a few seconds before he shouted again, "Mum!"

So shrill Vicky lashed out without thinking. She caught the boy's small hand and knocked the phone from it. The handset hit the hard ground with a *crack* that echoed in the tight alleyway. When Flynn stared at Vicky, his entire body slumped, she said, "You were making too much noise. Do you want to give us away?"

Flynn opened his mouth to reply but before he could get the words out, Brendan's deep voice echoed in the tight space. "Too late for that, my pretties. Did you *really* think you could get away from me?"

When Vicky peered around the corner, she saw the dirty man just metres from them as he limped up the alley.

Chapter Twenty-Nine

Although dark that evening, Rhys didn't need much light to comprehend what was behind them. The thin sliver of moon painted a silver highlight over what looked like thousands, maybe tens of thousands of heads moving at a steady jog. Although uncoordinated, they travelled as an army hell-bent on destruction. This world would be theirs. With the strength drained from his legs, Rhys froze as he watched the sheer force that bore down on them.

Blind because of the dark, Rhys slipped off the first branch and landed awkwardly. He whacked his shin and the sharp sting ran straight to his stomach. A deep breath and he continued down.

On his way to the bottom he misjudged where every branch would be. Each slip resulted in another whack and another instant bruise.

When he got close to the ground, Rhys slipped again. The next branch caught him with an uppercut beneath his chin and fire roared through his tongue as he bit into it. Stars swam in his vision and the metallic taste of blood filled his mouth. An angry pulse throbbed in the cut. He spat out the contents of his mouthful and continued down.

With the ground just a few metres away, he jumped. Another branch lifted his shirt up and raked his back. He wanted to rub the burn but he didn't have time. When he landed next to Larissa he said, "We've got to go. *Now!*"

While he heaved for breaths, Rhys felt the wide-eyed scrutiny from his ex-wife.

"What did you see?" she asked.

With blood in his mouth, there was no good way to rehydrate his throat as he moved off and croaked, "We've … got to … go … now."

Larissa followed him.

About twenty metres down the road, Larissa asked again. "What did you see, Rhys?"

Another deep breath and he finally found his words. "A fuck load of diseased,"—he paused—"and they're running this way. I don't think we can outpace them forever, but maybe we can get to Biggin Hill before them."

After she'd looked behind, Larissa swallowed and nodded. "Okay, let's speed it up."

With the city aglow on their right, Rhys searched and saw the sign on their left; the next exit led to Biggin Hill. A check behind and although he saw nothing, he heard them for sure, the groans of torment … of agony … of *hunger*.

The pair ran up the slip road and followed the signs to Biggin Hill. "I don't know what we'll do if we bump into more of them up here," Rhys said.

Larissa shook her head. "We can't think like that. We just need to keep going."

The groans behind them got louder with every step. "I can't

keep this up," Rhys said. "Biggin Hill's too far. We need to do something different. We're not going to outrun them."

When Larissa pointed, Rhys looked over and saw it as well, a car park full of cars. One of the overflow car parks for Summit City, it served as parking for those who'd yet to be given a permit to get into the city. They left their cars here and got a bus into work. Rhys looked at it and frowned. "What's your point?"

Larissa didn't reply. Instead, she ran at the car park and Rhys followed.

The wall around the outside stood less than a metre high. Enough to stop the cars from being driven out, it didn't need to be any higher. Larissa hurdled it and Rhys followed behind much slower. He winced as he stepped over the low barrier.

When the screams behind sounded louder than ever, Rhys looked and saw a few of the diseased at the front of the pack. "Larissa," he said. When she looked at him, he pointed over his shoulder.

Once she saw them, she instantly dropped to the ground.

Rhys did the same and hit the road so hard it stung his elbows and knees; like he needed any more fucking bruises.

They rolled under one of the cars in the lot.

Closer than they'd been in years, Rhys lay so near to Larissa he felt her body heat. The strong smell of oil surrounded them as they both recovered from the short run. "So what's your plan?" Rhys asked.

Larissa raised her eyebrows. "I hadn't really thought it through. I knew we needed somewhere to hide and this seemed like as good a place as any."

"Are you fucking *kidding* me? I would have been better up the tree. At least we know the diseased can't climb. If they see us here we're fucked." More blood had run into Rhys' mouth. The rich metallic taste flipped a heave through his stomach. After turning his tongue against itself to probe the slimy cut, he spat on the ground next to him.

For a few seconds, Larissa watched where he'd spat with a look of disgust before she said, "What else could we do? We tried running and they've caught up. Your plan to keep moving hasn't worked. At least they haven't seen us yet, and we're not far from the airport."

"We *hope* they haven't seen us, you mean."

Larissa turned away from Rhys.

As Rhys lay there, he focused on slowing his breaths and watched the first of the diseased appear. He expected bloody eyes to be down at his level and for hundreds of pairs of hands to clasp around his ankles at any moment.

But it didn't happen.

Within what felt like no more than a minute, hundreds of feet moved past them at a jog. From where Rhys lay, they looked like normal people. Apart from the occasional trainer with blood smeared on it, none of them looked infected. It seemed like a ridiculous predicament to find themselves in. But to be fair to Larissa what other choice did they have but to hide under the car? That, however, didn't change the fact that they needed to get to the airport soon.

When Rhys felt Larissa shake next to him, he rolled over and tapped on her slim shoulder. "Are you okay?" he asked in a whisper.

She turned around and her eyes were bloodshot. Her damp face glistened with tears. "We've let our boy down. We've come this far only to let him down." Her lip buckled as she shook her head. "I don't want to imagine a life where I'll never see him again."

The flow of diseased that passed the car thickened. They couldn't lie there and wait it out. If they went that route, they'd be waiting all day. A shake of his head and Rhys said, "Me either. It's not going to happen though. Come on, we can work this out. We can find a way."

Chapter Thirty

About thirty minutes ago

Brendan's deep laugh echoed off the walls of the alleyway. "You thought you could get away from *me*?" He continued to laugh, his mania flitting through the changing tone. "From *me*?!"

Vicky watched the wounded man for a few more seconds before she shoved Flynn down the alley.

When they got to the wall at the end, she kneeled down so she was at eye level with him and gripped both of his slim shoulders. "Now, Flynn, I know this man. I know he'll never give up. I need to send you over this wall while I deal with him."

Flynn shook his head and looked from one of her eyes to the other. His breath sped up and he trembled in her grip. "No, I can't go over there *alone*. Please don't make me."

Vicky looked behind to see Brendan and his evil grin as he got closer. She turned back to Flynn. "I *need* you out of the way. If you're here, you'll take some of my attention away from dealing with him and I may fail. I have a better chance without you around." Vicky lifted her ear to the air. "I can't hear any of the diseased over there. There's also something else I need you to do for me."

Although he looked at her, Flynn didn't respond.

"I need you to wait for five minutes and no longer, okay? If I'm not over this wall in five minutes' time, you need to head south. Your mum and dad will be at Biggin Hill Airport so you need to go that way."

A violent tremble ran though the boy and he shook his head. "I don't know where that is." His eyes glazed.

"Back past the drawbridge. Back the way we came."

The sound of Brendan's laugh got closer and he called out. "Little pig, little pig, let me in."

A chill snapped through Vicky and she lifted Flynn up. The boy felt heavier than he ever had, as if her guilt made him harder to pick up. She lifted him onto her shoulders and walked closer to the wall. "I need you to stand on my shoulders, Flynn."

The boy shook his entire body rather than just his head. "I can't. I can't do this."

A lump, too big to swallow, swelled in Vicky's throat. She had to fight to get her words out. "You'll *die* if you don't."

So close now Vicky heard the sound of Brendan dragging his foot up the alley. She turned to the large man. Limp or not, the sight of him damn near paralysed her with fear.

"Hurry up, Flynn." Vicky strained to lift him higher and she felt his little feet find her shoulders. "Now reach up to the top of the wall."

When she glanced up, brick dust, or something similar, rained down and stung her eyes. She had to blink several times for her vision to clear. As Flynn reached for the top of the wall, she grabbed each of his feet and fought the weakness in her arms to push him even higher.

Flynn grabbed the top and pulled himself up. He sat up there for a second and peered over the other side.

"How does it look?" Vicky asked. "Any diseased over there?"

But Flynn didn't look at her. Instead, he focused on Brendan who had moved to within about five metres of the pair.

"Flynn! Are there any diseased over there?"

The boy looked back over and shook his head. "No."

"Good. Now jump and go and hide." Her words cracked in her throat at the desperation of their lot. "I'll be over in five minutes."

Flynn lifted his leg over the wall and Vicky watched him through her watery eyes. He still had the police baton in his tiny grip. Tears ran hot streaks down her cheeks as she saw the embodiment of innocence vanish over the top. The boy didn't stand a chance. Baton or not, he probably wouldn't be able to beat any of the diseased. But she didn't have any other choice. The wall stood too high for her to climb and no way could she beat Brendan. At least with the boy over the other side, she may be able to do something. Highly unlikely, but some chance was better than none.

With Brendan just a few metres away, Vicky snapped her telescopic baton open and blinked her tears away. She clenched her jaw and stared at the wall of a man.

Chapter Thirty-One

Rhys laid his cheek against the cold road beneath the car. The diseased shuffled past them on either side, the air thick with their rancid reek. There seemed to be no end to the dense crowd. If they waited too much longer, they'd miss Flynn and Vicky completely. Impatience twitched through Rhys and the desire to move sat balled in his leg muscles.

After he'd rolled over onto his back, Rhys rested his head against the hard road surface and looked up at the underside of the car. A large panel covered the bottom and was dirty from where all the crud on the road had kicked up beneath it.

A deep breath and he let out a long and slow sigh. They'd come all this way to get fucked over at the last minute. Without a plan, they'd have to remain stuck beneath the car until the fuckers passed. They'd be there for hours.

When Larissa shifted next to Rhys, he looked across to see her pick up a rock about the size of a tennis ball. She motioned for him to move out of her way but he resisted. Her next action could kill them both. When he looked into her green eyes, she glared back at him. It seemed clear that nothing would stop her.

Rhys shifted down toward the back of the car.

The smell of the dirty exhaust fought for his attention over the reek of the diseased, and Rhys tried his best to breathe through his mouth. Although better than rot, he'd rather not have either scent around him.

Now he'd moved low enough he watched Larissa press her cheek to the ground and look along the bottom of the cars as if to check how level the road was. She clutched the rock in one hand, pulled it back close to her chest, and frowned with concentration.

No, surely she won't ...

But before Rhys could stop her, she slid the rock away from her like a curling stone. It missed the first lot of legs immediately next to them and shot beneath the first car.

Rhys' world slipped into slow motion as he watched it pass beneath three more cars. He flinched every time it narrowly avoided a diseased foot and listened to the dry *whoosh* as it slid along the ground. When it came to the fifth car, it hit its alloy wheel with a bright *ting*. The sound seemed to ring all the way to London.

As one, the diseased halted and Rhys nearly pissed himself.

Screams came to life around them and the pack sped up and changed direction as they cut across the car park and headed toward the sound.

After about thirty seconds, Rhys looked the other way, in the direction of the woods. The amount of diseased on that side had thinned considerably. A second later, Larissa poked her head out from under the car and commando crawled to the vehicle next to them.

With his heart in his throat and his mouth so dry he nearly heaved, Rhys gulped, rolled over onto his front, and shuffled along the ground after her.

Once beneath the next car, another rush of diseased sped past them. Surely they only had a short window before the creatures realised they had nothing to chase after, not that he needed to tell Larissa to hurry.

With his veins flooded with adrenaline, Rhys watched Larissa repeat the process to get to the next car along. One more and maybe she could run to the woods.

Rhys followed, but just as he stuck his head out, the foot of a diseased slammed down in front of him. Fear stabbed through his chest and he snapped his head back as the clumsy monster shuffled past.

As he lay beneath the car, he shook and he waited for the call that would give him away to the other diseased.

But it never came.

Rhys watched the feet that nearly stood on him. They headed toward the sound Larissa's thrown rock had made.

Another check and Rhys saw it was clear. He followed after Larissa again.

Larissa had already moved to the final vehicle in the lot. A Ford truck, it had a little more room beneath it than the other vehicles.

Rhys followed quickly after.

When he got across, Rhys looked at the woodland just ten metres away and gasped for breath. Not that the escape had been particularly strenuous, but it had fried his nerves.

Larissa studied the underside of the truck and spoke in a

whisper. "I refuse to give up on our boy." As she said this, she moved down toward the back of the vehicle.

A round plastic panel held the spare tyre beneath the bottom of the truck. Larissa started to unscrew it.

Rhys shifted so he lay next to her and pushed against the panel. Whatever she'd decided to do, she needed help.

The screw came more easily without the weight of the tyre against it, and Larissa spun it free.

After she'd pulled the screw away, Rhys let the plastic cover slide down and took the weight of the heavy tyre with him. They didn't need the noise of that to pull the diseased back over to them

Larissa moved back and Rhys let the tyre down to the ground, his arms sore from the weight of it. A glance across at the diseased and he saw they'd all stopped near the rock Larissa had thrown. How long could that amuse them for before they worked it out?

When Larissa pulled the tools away from the inside of the wheel, they made the slightest *pop*.

Rhys held his breath and watched the mob's feet over by the rock.

None of them seemed to hear it.

Larissa continued on. She pulled the jack and the tyre iron free and found a screwdriver.

When she held it up at Rhys and grinned, he didn't know what to say. Unless it was a sonic screwdriver, what did she hope to do with it?

After she'd gently discarded all of the other bits, Larissa crawled over to the edge of the car by the woodland area. She looked both up and down the road, and then up at the side of the truck.

When she came back in, she grabbed Rhys' arm and spoke in a whisper. "This is our opportunity. There's no diseased this close to the woods. I need you to trust and follow me, okay?"

If it meant they had a chance to save Flynn, Rhys would crawl through hellfire. He nodded.

Larissa rolled out from under the vehicle and Rhys followed her.

Exposed without the truck for cover, Rhys hopped up into a crouch and looked up and down the lot. The outer two rows of cars had no diseased around them anymore. While there had been, and continued to be, plenty of the fuckers in the car park, the road that ran parallel to it was packed dense with bodies. They'd only had to deal with the overflow so far.

Rhys watched as Larissa wedged the screwdriver into the petrol cap cover on the side of the truck. She banged it once with the heel of her hand to force the blade in place. She then pulled on the screwdriver until a slight *ping* rang out. The cap cover snapped open. Rhys flinched in anticipation of an alarm, but none came. They dodged a bullet there. She couldn't have known that would happen.

The temperature had dropped and fear had Rhys in its icy grip as he looked around. The noise they'd made hadn't been loud, but it sounded like a gunshot when silence meant the difference between life and death.

When Rhys glanced back at Larissa, he watched her unscrew the petrol cap and pull it free. She then pulled her top off so she stood there in just a bra. Despite the tension of the situation,

Rhys' eyes wandered to her breasts. Familiar, but completely forbidden, he stared at the body he once knew so well. When he looked back up to see her eyes on him, he winced an apology, but she didn't seem to care.

She rolled her shirt up and stuffed the arm end into the petrol tank.

She fed the rolled up garment in until just a few inches poked out.

The smell of petrol fumes wafted out of the tank and Rhys' mouth watered. A smell he'd never tire of and a damn sight better than the reek of disease.

Larissa opened up the Zippo lighter she'd found in the pocket of the man in the town. She struck the wheel and the flame shimmered in the slight breeze. After she'd checked around, she lit the small part of her top that still poked out.

Rhys didn't need to be told what to do next.

As one, the pair watched the flame bite into the shirt before they both turned and ran for the woods.

Chapter Thirty-Two

About twenty minutes ago

Tears ran warm tracks down Vicky's cheeks as she stared at the crazed man who came toward her. A twisted and hellish version of the person she'd loved, he seemed to fill the tight alleyway with his wide and tall frame. Her pulse raced, her throat dried, and she shook where she stood. Her life would end in that alley, but what about Flynn? Six years old and she'd just condemned him to death. So much for the promise she'd made to Rhys. Hopefully when he fell to the diseased, the pain would be nothing compared to what Brendan had in mind for him.

With her baton held in a tight grip, Vicky watched the lunatic limp toward her. She looked down at his thigh and saw his jeans were soaked from where he'd clearly lost a lot of blood. Another look at the man and she suddenly saw his crazed glare as something else. Sunken sockets in his pale face, she then noticed the shake that ran through his weak body. Maybe he didn't have long left. Maybe he only kept going for revenge, and once he'd achieved that he'd fall flat. Maybe she *could* get out.

As if he knew she'd seen his frailty, Brendan laughed. The deep boom of his voice echoed in the alley and vibrated against her chest. "When we pulled away from The Alpha Tower after we'd freed the virus, I thought I'd seen the back of Summit City. But then we found out about how the city had been set to incinerate. You *knew* about that, didn't you?"

Vicky shook her head. "No."

Brendan said something Vicky didn't understand. It sounded Chinese. He smiled. "Didn't know I was fluent in Chinese, did you? There's a lot about me that you *don't* know. I'll repeat what I just said, shall I?"

She gulped but said nothing.

"I said, 'don't lie to me, *bitch*'."

Vicky stared at the man and clenched her jaw tight. She didn't need to argue with him. It didn't matter if he believed her or not.

After several deep breaths, his brow soaked in sweat, Brendan said, "They sent me back to override the order. Just in case I didn't manage to do it, they airlifted the diseased from the city and dropped them first in London, and then around the country. They even sent a few over to mainland Europe. That's why the streets are infected now."

The cries of the diseased filled the air and Vicky kept her ears open to the noise. A spike in their frenzied calls would tell her that maybe Flynn had fallen. Nothing yet. She stared at Brendan. "Good job they did that, eh?"

"Huh?"

"Well, you clearly *failed* in your task. The city has gone up in flames."

"Your new boyfriend stopped me. He tied me in the room with a lab coat bound to the handles. But I managed to pull a strip of metal away from the point where the bottom of the wall met the ground. It was slim and sharp enough to both slip through the gap in the door and cut the lab coat."

With only a couple of metres between them now, Brendan continued to shuffle forward. When Vicky noticed his piercing eyes roll in his head, she drew another deep breath. She could get past him. The longer this played out, the weaker he became.

"You know …" Brendan had to pause to catch his breath. "I would have left you alone if Rhys hadn't been such a cunt. If I'd have been allowed to complete my task and get out of the city, I would have done that and moved on. But because of Rhys, I'm going to make sure *everyone* he holds dear pays. You first, then his little shit of a boy. Then I'll hunt Rhys down."

The man obviously didn't have it in him. Despite the front, Brendan had no fight left.

"I'm going to torture his little boy when I find him, diseased or not. Nice trick sending him over the wall, although I doubt he'll last two minutes on his own. Even if he does manage to hide from the diseased, I'll find him and make him suffer."

When just a metre separated the pair, Brendan lunged at Vicky. He moved as if in slow motion, his injury slowing him down. In one fluid movement, Vicky dodged his long arms and jabbed her baton into his thigh.

Brendan yelled out and fell to the ground. With his hands clamped to his leg, he roared like the diseased that surrounded them.

Without the room to swing her baton Vicky jabbed him

again, this time across his chin. When Brendan fell to the ground, she hopped over him and ran off down the alley.

***

As soon as she'd left the alley, Vicky found Flynn on the side of the road. He'd huddled in a ball as he waited. Good job she'd come out and not Brendan.

When she went over and touched his shoulder, he jumped and snapped his head up. Bloodshot eyes stared up at her, red from tears rather than the disease.

The groans of perpetual suffering came at them from every direction. Before long, the diseased would find them again.

A quick glance around and Vicky saw a truck with its door wide open. The lights were on as if it had been abandoned.

She pulled on one of Flynn's tiny hands. "Come on, we need to get out of here."

At first, the boy didn't budge. Shock and fear seemed to have paralysed him. After another tug, he got to his feet.

The sounds of the diseased grew louder so Vicky picked the boy up. Too heavy to carry any great distance, she managed to lift him over to the truck. A quick check and she saw the key sat in the ignition like she hoped it would be. She twisted the key and the large vehicle shook and then roared to life. After she'd dragged Flynn around to the passenger seat, she slammed the door. When she looked up, she saw a horde round the bend at a full sprint.

She ran around to her side of the truck, hopped in, slammed the door, and hit the central lock. Not that it would do any good against the mob. They'd tear though concrete to get at their prey.

As the diseased closed in on them, Vicky threw the truck into first gear and accelerated away.

The mob filled her rear-view mirror for a few seconds, but as she picked up speed, they grew smaller.

After she'd negotiated the tight streets and swerved around the occasional diseased, Vicky got out onto the open seven-lane highway. She rested a hand on Flynn's knee. "It's okay. We've left the bad man and the diseased behind. It's okay. We'll find your mum and dad, I promise." She squeezed his leg again. "I *promise*."

Chapter Thirty-Three

As Rhys and Larissa reached the tree line, the truck went up with a loud *whoomph* behind them. Seconds later, a hard gust of hot air shoved Rhys in the back and he stumbled. The rapid change in temperature brought a layer of sweat to the surface of Rhys' skin. When he looked at Larissa, he saw how the light glistened off her damp skin too.

Once they'd entered the dark cover of the trees, they both stopped and peered out. Rhys watched the truck they'd ignited burn on its own. As one, the diseased descended on the blazing wreck. The bright flames picked out their twisted faces and snapping jaws.

The first of the diseased reached the truck and screamed as they caught on fire. "What the fuck?" Rhys said.

Larissa shifted to see out of the trees too. "They're not running away."

And they weren't. As one fell to the flames, three more ploughed into the vehicle.

The ignited diseased bridged the gap to the next car and it caught on fire too. A few seconds later, Rhys flinched at the blinding flash and second loud *whoomph*.

This time, the gust of hot air brought the sweet and fatty smell of seared flesh with it, and Rhys vomited a small amount of bile into his mouth. The sharp and bitter kick twisted his face and he spat on the ground, but the acidic burn remained in his throat.

A continuous monotone ring hummed in Rhys' ears from the loud explosion as he watched the car burn, and he blinked repeatedly to take the flashes from his vision.

Before he'd fully recovered his sight, another two cars blew up and the ground shook. The double explosion pushed out another hot gust that rushed toward them and blew the hair back from Rhys' forehead.

When Larissa tugged on his arm, Rhys saw she'd stepped farther back into the woods and he let her pull him in with her.

By the time the next explosion happened, Rhys had turned his back on it. If he stood there and watched every one of the explosions, his night vision would be shot to pieces, although maybe he didn't need night vision with the bright glow from the car park. Another several cars went up and drowned out the sounds of the diseased as they burned alive.

The cars continued to blow. Three, four, five, six at a time and each explosion rang louder than the last. They lit up the night and shook the ground.

"When shall we move on?" Larissa said as another three or four cars exploded.

Despite the ring in his ears, Rhys just about heard her. He shook his head. "Not yet. If we can wait this out then maybe it'll kill all the diseased and we can get back on the road."

Rhys watched Larissa open her mouth to reply, but the screech of tyres cut her dead.

When Rhys looked up, he saw a truck. It came from the same direction they'd come from and it had lost control as it snaked down the road toward them.

When the truck got closer, the bright flames showed Rhys two people in the cab: a woman and a boy. "Oh *fuck*!"

His entire body tensed when the truck finally lost it, flipped, and went into a barrel roll. The large vehicle crunched and popped as it lost its wing mirrors, panels dented, and the windows broke. After a particularly loud *pop* that had obviously put a window out completely, Rhys heard the scream of a little boy.

The truck came to rest against the small wall that surrounded the lot. It lay on its side just feet away from the burning cars. Panic stole his breaths and he only realised how hard he gripped Larissa's arm when he saw her wince. He eased off and said, "That's Flynn and Vicky."

"How do you know?"

A wall of flames separated the burning diseased from the wrecked truck. It would hold them back for a time. A line of explosions then ripped through the car park, away from Vicky and Flynn. It took out yet more diseased, but they continued to flock to the flames.

"Well?" Larissa said.

"Oh, sorry," Rhys said as he watched the chaos. His eyes stung from the light and he sweated more than ever. "I just know it's them." He stepped out of the trees and the heat pushed against him. More cars exploded away from them, but all of the cars close to the first one had already gone up in flames; all except the truck with his boy inside.

The screech of a second set of tyres stopped Rhys in his tracks. It too came from the same way Vicky and Flynn had, and it too cannoned toward the parked cars. It seemed to have its sights set on Vicky and Flynn.

It took for Larissa to speak for Rhys to realise she'd walked out of the trees with him and stood by his side. "Then who's that?"

Chapter Thirty-Four

About fifteen minutes ago

The entire truck shook when Vicky hit a diseased. Flynn screamed next to her. His shrill cry stung her ears. She'd seen this one coming too late so she hit it head on. It rolled up over the bonnet and cracked the windscreen much like the one they'd hit in the car had.

Adrenaline ran a wobble through Vicky's arms, and no matter how tightly she gripped the wheel, she swerved from side to side on the wide road.

On their right, Summit City still burned. On their left, the dark woodland peered out at them.

They hit another diseased. Another thud shook through the truck and the diseased flew off to one side.

"I'm scared, Vicky."

Vicky reached across and squeezed Flynn's arm. "Don't be, honey, everything's okay. This is a big, strong truck, and it'll get us to where we need to be. Don't worry. Remember, in *Call of Duty: Zombies*, the idea is to kill the zombies. Think of the points we'd get for driving into them."

Flynn remained curled in a ball, his feet pulled up onto the seat with his heels pressed into his bottom, but he lifted his head and looked out of the window at the road. "Kinda hard to see now, isn't it?"

Cracks ran all the way across the windscreen, but Vicky still managed to see the next diseased. At the last moment, she swerved to avoid it.

Flynn laughed.

"What's so funny?"

The boy relaxed his tense little frame and pointed out in front of them. "That was an easy fifty points and you *completely* missed it. I think *I* should drive."

"You cheeky ..." Vicky left it there and the smallest hint of a smile lifted her lips.

When they passed the drawbridge, Vicky slowed down a little and frowned hard as she stared into the dark. The police car remained in the same place, though that was hardly a surprise considering she'd thrown the keys away earlier. The booth that controlled the bridge also remained unoccupied. Not that it mattered. The orange glow from Summit City showed it still burned, so even if someone did lower it now all they'd find would be ash. Vicky put her foot down again and the large diesel engine pulled them on.

***

When they came to the exit signpost for Biggin Hill, Vicky turned to Flynn. The boy had his feet on the ground now and had relaxed a lot more. They'd not hit, or even seen a diseased for the past half a mile or so.

The cracks in the glass dragged lines of light across Vicky's vision, but she didn't need to see that well as long as she stayed on the wide road. "We're close to the airport now, Flynn. Don't worry, we'll find your mum and da—"

Before Vicky could finish, she saw the headlights on the road behind her and a chill snapped her body taut. It could have been anyone, but Vicky knew. "*Brendan*? Not again."

The mention of the man's name caused Flynn to straighten in his seat, turn around, and look out of the back window. "Is it the *man*, Vicky? The *zombie* man?"

For a moment, Vicky didn't reply. Instead, she watched the lights as the car behind gained on them. When would he give up? She finally said, "Yep, it's him."

"Oh God." Flynn lifted his feet back onto the seat and wrapped his arms around his knees to pull them in closer. "What does he *want* from us? Why won't he leave us alone? You won't leave me on my own again, will you?"

The last question stabbed Vicky's heart and she didn't reply. Instead, she put her foot down and squinted through the broken windscreen. When Brendan flicked on his full-beam headlights, she frowned harder than before as she tried to see in the dark.

Suddenly an explosion lit up in front of them. The cracks on the windscreen spread the bright light all the way across the window and Vicky swerved. Several more explosions came to life about twenty metres away and completely blinded Vicky.

In her attempt to bring the vehicle back under control, she snaked from side to side. A glance behind and she saw the bright light of Brendan's car.

Another explosion in front and Vicky hit the brakes. Regardless of what happened behind them, they couldn't drive straight into the fire in front. But she hit the brakes too hard. The truck tilted up onto one side before it flipped and went into a barrel roll.

Although Vicky tried to reach out to Flynn, within seconds, she'd lost her bearings as the car rolled over and over. Each time, despite her seatbelt being on, a moment of weightlessness was followed by a loud bang and a heavy impact through a different part of her body. She whacked her knees on the steering wheel, her shoulder against the driver's side window, and the air flew from her chest from the pressure of her belt when she jolted forward.

On the next moment of weightlessness, she reached out to Flynn again but grasped only thin air. A bright light then punched through her vision when she whacked her head. A bell rang in her ears and her world went dark.

***

Groggy from the crash, Vicky heard a loud *bang* next to her and opened her eyes. Her seat belt held her in place as the truck lay on its side. The weight of her entire body rested on her left ribs. Her door pointed toward the dark sky.

Flames roared next to the truck and had turned the temperature up by what felt like a thousand degrees. Sweat had turned her entire body slick. When she looked down, she saw Flynn. His door was lowest to the ground, and he was lying unconscious against it.

Another loud *bang* and the glass from the door on Vicky's

side rained down on her. She shook the window fragments away and looked up to see Brendan standing above her.

Vicky shook her head but before she could speak, Brendan shouted at her. "Thought you'd gotten away from me? Well, guess again, *bitch*." Brendan leaned down into the car and cut off her air with a tight grip around her throat.

Chapter Thirty-Five

Unable to breathe, stars flashed in Vicky's vision as Brendan squeezed tighter. She flapped her hand in the direction of the seat belt release, but couldn't find it.

With her eyes on Brendan, she saw the man's teeth as he clenched his jaw. Veins stood out on his forehead and saliva dripped from his mouth. A large globule landed just below her left eye. If he squeezed much harder, he'd break her windpipe for sure.

Woozy from the lack of oxygen Vicky fought against her body's desire to fall limp. Whatever happened, she needed to get Flynn out before the truck blew up.

The heat from the flames pushed against Vicky's face and turned the air stuffy. If the lack of oxygen didn't drag her under, the heat would. Vicky gave up on the seatbelt, reached up, and grabbed Brendan's wrist. One last chance to get out of the situation, she dug her nails in hard.

Brendan's eyes flew wide, but he didn't let go, he squeezed harder instead.

Darkness narrowed Vicky's vision and she could only hear

the sound of herself choking. And then, just before complete blackout, Brendan let go.

A hungry gasp of air and Vicky looked up to see Brendan had gone. Seconds later, the face of a woman appeared. Although Vicky opened and closed her mouth several times, she couldn't get her words out. She continued to gasp for air. Who the fuck was she?

The woman looked past her at Flynn, who lay crumpled at the bottom of the car. "*Flynn.*"

Of course! Vicky finally coughed a word out. "Larissa?"

The woman pointed down the vehicle. "Get me my boy. Get him before this truck blows up."

Still groggy from the crash and with a headache pounding in her temples, Vicky found the seatbelt release this time and popped the button. She managed to catch the steering wheel as she fell and stopped herself just short of landing on the boy by pulling her legs up to her chest.

Although knocked out, Flynn's body moved with his shallow breaths. A gentle tap on the side of his face and he opened his eyes.

"Hey," said Vicky, her voice no more than a quiet croak, "look who's here."

The dazed boy turned and looked up. He drew a sharp intake of breath. "Mum?"

"Oh, Flynn," Larissa replied. "Flynn, I'm so glad you're okay."

Vicky watched the woman as she cried and leaned into the car. Vicky then lifted Flynn up so his mum could take him. After she'd dragged Flynn out of the car, Vicky stepped up on the handbrake and poked her head out of the driver's side window.

An entire car park of cars burned in front of them. The flames seemed dangerously close. Close enough that she could smell her own singed hair and the heat prickled her skin.

After she'd boosted herself out of the truck, Vicky jumped down. When she hit the ground, the impact stung her knees and she nearly fell over. Larissa and Flynn headed over to the woodland area, but Vicky saw Brendan and Rhys locked in a battle on the hard road. The scream of the diseased roared behind them. Before long, they'd be swarmed by the horrible fuckers.

Vicky removed the telescopic baton from her pocket and snapped it open. She ran as fast as her weak legs could carry her, wound back, and cracked Brendan with the baton. The first swing hit his shoulder, and it did enough for the big man to scream and let go of Rhys.

When Rhys jumped away, Vicky clenched her jaw and swung the baton into Brendan's stomach.

The shrieks from the darkness behind them got louder.

Vicky drove another blow to Brendan's side and he wheezed as if winded. After a deep breath, she hit him as hard as she could on the bloody patch on his right thigh.

Brendan screamed like he'd been set fire to, and the diseased behind answered his call in kind. Although Vicky wanted to hit him again, Rhys tugged on her arm and dragged her away. "Come on, Vick, they'll be on us soon. We have to go now."

***

Vicky, Rhys, Flynn, and Larissa hid in the darkness of the trees and watched as shadows emerged from the road behind Brendan. The burning cars gave off enough light to expose their shuffling forms. One of the lead diseased spotted Brendan. It called out and a mob descended on him.

The first one to reach him bit hard into the side of Brendan's face and the man screamed so loud it echoed through the night. Another one arrived a second later and bit his leg.

Drained and with the heat of the fire pressed against her, Vicky's vision blurred as she stood there. She needed to see this. The man she loved and hated had met his end, but she had to make sure.

When she felt a tug on her arm, Vicky turned to Rhys. He, Larissa, and Flynn all looked at her as Rhys said, "Come on, Vicky, it's over. It's done."

A deep sigh and Vicky nodded. He was right. It was done.

She followed the family as they ducked into the darkness of the woods.

When they were no more than ten metres in, a loud explosion shook the ground beneath their feet. Vicky turned around to see the truck she'd driven smothered in flames. She watched it for a second before she followed after the other three again.

Chapter Thirty-Six

In the cover of the trees, Vicky stood back while Rhys and Larissa hugged their boy.

"Oh, my God," Larissa said as she seemed to purposely turn her back on Vicky, "I've missed you *so* much. I'm so glad you're okay. Mummy's never going to leave you again."

Smothered by his parents, it seemed that Flynn could barely move as they both held him tight.

There had to be a perfectly rational reason for Larissa to be topless, save for a bra, but now wasn't the time to address it. Instead, Vicky stood back and waited, the smell of tree sap a welcome change from that of the diseased. The sound of the creatures still called out close behind them. Having taken Brendan down, they seemed to be on the lookout for something else to attack.

"You must have been petrified, mate," Rhys said as he ruffled his boy's hair.

After he'd nodded, Flynn pointed at Vicky. "It was okay though, Vicky really looked after me. She said we should imagine we were playing *Call of Duty: Zombies*, so we did. How many points did we score, Vicky?"

In spite of everything that had happened, Vicky smiled as she looked at the boy. Her voice still croaked from where she'd been strangled. "It had to be a new high score for sure. We beat it, Flynn." She then held her hand out for Flynn to give her a high five. His tiny hand hit hers as she repeated, "We *beat* it."

The ice that Larissa had projected at Vicky seemed to melt and the topless woman managed a smile at her.

Before they could say anything to one another, Rhys pointed a thumb over his shoulder. "I still think we should head to Biggin Hill Airport. We need to get away from here as soon as possible. Maybe we can catch a private jet before it takes off? Besides," he said as he looked back to where they'd just come from, "if we wait around here, those things are bound to find us."

Without another word, the group set off in the direction of the airport.

***

They may not have been able to see them, but the sound of the diseased served as a constant reminder that they hadn't shaken them. Vicky kept looking over her shoulder, expecting to see their clumsy forms amongst the trees. Maybe no more than a coincidence, but the pack on their tail seemed to be just that; on their tail. Maybe they'd seen or even smelled them. Or maybe it was just bad luck that they'd chosen the same path.

They'd started out at a fast walk, but the four of them gradually picked their pace up until they moved at a jog. Rhys had thrown Flynn over his shoulder and carried him like a fireman would.

Vicky's exhausted muscles hurt and she had to dig deep to keep her limbs working, but she pushed on anyway and kept up with the others. No doubt they felt much like she did. Their pained grimaces certainly suggested they did.

***

When they reached the edge of the woodland and with the airport in sight, Vicky looked at the group. The strained relationship between Rhys and Larissa had obviously been healed. An apocalypse seemed like a great way to gain some perspective.

Before she spoke, she listened to the call of the diseased. The murmur of suffering and discontent rode on the breeze. The smell of burned rubber joined the sounds as the car park behind them continued to glow in the night. The diseased sounded far enough away. "I think if we're going to go for it, it needs to be now," Vicky said.

Each person in the group nodded.

"The terminal for the private jets is on the other side of the airport. We'll need to be quick because we'll be out in open space when we leave the cover of the trees."

Again, the other three nodded their agreement with Vicky.

After a deep breath, Vicky counted them down. "Okay, three, two, one …" She sprinted from the cover of the woods and heard the footsteps as the others followed her.

But the second they stepped out into the open, a diseased scream called through the night.

When Vicky looked over her shoulder, she saw them. A crowd bigger than any she'd seen before descended on them.

They filled the road and the burning cars behind showed her more of them than she wanted the see. The glazed look in their wide eyes spoke of their desire to get at the four.

They had no chance of outrunning the creatures to the airport terminal. They needed a change of plan.

About twenty metal shipping containers lay dotted about in the car park of one of the empty units. Despite the poor light, Vicky saw the ladder propped up against the side of one.

She headed for it. In their current predicament they needed higher ground above all else.

Vicky arrived at the container first and her lungs burned as she climbed the ladder with wobbly legs.

Before she'd gotten to the top Larissa had arrived and followed her up.

Rhys brought up the rear and put Flynn on the ladder first. Vicky watched him bounce on the spot as his boy climbed. The diseased bore down on him.

Rhys jumped on the ladder a second later. As he made his way up, Vicky saw the diseased moments before it grabbed his ankle.

Rhys kicked the thing in the face and knocked it backwards. When it fell on its arse Rhys quickened his climb.

By the time Rhys had reached the top, the thing had gotten back to its feet. Before it could do anything else, Vicky, clumsy with the adrenaline that ran through her blood, lifted the ladder. She nearly fell when the lead diseased grabbed the bottom rung and tugged her down, but Larissa pulled Vicky back to keep her from dropping into the diseased below.

Gritting her teeth, Vicky yanked the ladder hard and

managed to rip it from the monster's grip.

After they'd pulled the ladder up onto the container with them, both Larissa and Rhys went to their boy again and Vicky watched the mob below.

The crowd seemed to double with each passing minute, and before long it felt like they wouldn't be able to see anything but the horrible fuckers.

Rhys eventually walked over to Vicky and stood next to her as he looked out over the crowd. He didn't speak for a few seconds, and then he finally said, "Thank you for bringing my boy back to me."

Vicky shrugged while she chewed the inside of her mouth.

After a weary sigh, Rhys nodded out at the gathering horde. "The bastards may not be able to climb, but how the fuck will we get out of this?"

Vicky gave him the only response she had. After a deep inhale where the reek of rotten death damn near choked her, she shrugged and said, "Fucked if I know."

Ends.

For my other titles - go to www.michaelrobertson.co.uk

About The Author

Michael Robertson has been a writer for many years and has had poetry and short stories published, most notably with HarperCollins. He first discovered his desire to write as a skinny weed-smoking seventeen-year-old badman who thought he could spit bars over drum and bass. Fortunately, that venture never left his best mate's bedroom and only a few people had to endure his musical embarrassment. He hasn't so much as looked at a microphone since. What the experience taught him was that he liked to write. So that's what he did.

After sending poetry to countless publications and receiving MANY rejection letters, he uttered the words, "That's it, I give up." The very next day, his first acceptance letter arrived in the post. He saw it as a sign that he would find his way in the world as a writer.

Over a decade and a half later, he now has a young family to inspire him and has decided to follow his joy with every ounce of his being. With the support of his amazing partner, Amy, he's managed to find the time to take the first step of what promises to be an incredible journey. Love, hope, and the need to eat get him out of bed every morning to spend a precious few hours pursuing his purpose.

If you want to connect with Michael:

Subscribe to my newsletter at –
www.michaelrobertson.co.uk

Email me at –
subscribers@michaelrobertson.co.uk

Follow me on Facebook at –
www.facebook.com/MichaelRobertsonAuthor

Twitter at –
@MicRobertson

Google Plus at –
plus.google.com/u/0/113009673177382863155/posts

OTHER AUTHORS UNDER THE SHIELD OF

SIXTH CYCLE

Nuclear war has destroyed human civilization. Captain Jake Phillips wakes into a dangerous new world, where he finds the remaining fragments of the population living in a series of strongholds, connected across the country. Uneasy alliances have maintained their safety, but things are about to change. — Discovery **leads to danger.** — Skye Reed, a tracker from the Omega stronghold, uncovers a threat that could spell the end for their fragile society. With friends and enemies revealing truths about the past, she will need to decide who to trust. — **Sixth Cycle** is a gritty post-apocalyptic story of survival and adventure.

Darren Wearmouth ~ Carl Sinclair

DEAD ISLAND: Operation Zulu

Ten years after the world was nearly brought to its knees by a zombie Armageddon, there is a race for the antidote! On a remote Caribbean island, surrounded by a horde of hungry living dead, a team of American and Australian commandos must rescue the Antidotes' scientist. Filled with zombies, guns, Russian bad guys, shady government types, serial killers and elevator muzak. Dead Island is an action packed blood soaked horror adventure.

Allen Gamboa

INVASION OF THE DEAD SERIES

This is the first book in a series of nine, about an ordinary bunch of friends, and their plight to survive an apocalypse in Australia. — Deep beneath defense headquarters in the Australian Capital Territory, the last ranking Army chief and a brilliant scientist struggle with answers to the collapse of the world, and the aftermath of an unprecedented virus. Is it a natural mutation, or does the infection contain — more sinister roots? — One hundred and fifty miles away, five friends returning from a month-long camping trip slowly discover that death has swept through the country. What greets them in a gradual revelation is an enemy beyond compare. — Armed with dwindling ammunition, the friends must overcome their disagreements, utilize their individual skills, and face unimaginable horrors as they battle to reach their hometown…

Owen Baillie

WHISKEY TANGO FOXTROT

Alone in a foreign land. The radio goes quiet while on convoy in Afghanistan, a lost patrol alone in the desert. With his unit and his home base destroyed, Staff Sergeant Brad Thompson suddenly finds himself isolated and in command of a small group of men trying to survive in the Afghan wasteland. **Every turn leads to danger**

The local population has been afflicted with an illness that turns them into rabid animals. They pursue him and his men at every corner and stop. Struggling to hold his team together and unite survivors, he must fight and evade his way to safety.

A fast paced zombie war story like no other.

W.J. Lundy

ZOMBIE RUSH

New to the Hot Springs PD Lisa Reynolds was not all that welcomed by her coworkers especially those who were passed over for the position. It didn't matter, her thirty days probation ended on the same day of the Z-poc's arrival. Overnight the world goes from bad to worse as thousands die in the initial onslaught. National Guard and regular military unit deployed the day before to the north leaves the city in mayhem. All directions lead to death until one unlikely candidate steps forward with a plan. A plan that became an avalanche raging down the mountain culminating in the salvation or destruction of them all.

Joseph Hansen

THE GATHERING HORDE

The most ambitious terrorist plot ever undertaken is about to be put into motion, releasing an unstoppable force against humanity. Ordinary people – A group of students celebrating the end of the semester, suburban and rural families – are about to themselves in the center of something that threatens the survival of the human species. As they battle the dead – and the living – it's going to take every bit of skill, knowledge and luck for them to survive in Zed's World.

Rich Baker

THE FORGOTTEN LAND

Sergeant Steve Golburn, an Australian Special Air Service veteran, is tasked with a dangerous mission in Iraq, deep behind enemy lines. When Steve's five man SAS patrol inadvertently spark a time portal, they find themselves in 10th century Viking Denmark. A place far more dangerous and lawless than modern Iraq. Join the SAS patrol on this action adventure into the depths of not only a hostile land, far away from the support of the Allied front line, but into another world…another time.

Keith McArdle

<<<<>>>>

Printed in Great Britain
by Amazon